THE TIDE'S TURN

rlotte Vale, Will Jervis and Andrew
comb were childhood friends, but when
lrew left Whitby for America, Charlotte
not know he was forced to leave
owing the death of a young woman.
When he returns she is overjoyed, and
mes Andrew will take over the family
shipping firm, but he seems more interested
in pleasure, leaving the running of the firm
to his sister Hester, assisted by Will. When
Andrew suddenly marries, and expects
Charlotte to become his wife's companion,
she is forced to question whether she really
knew Andrew at all.

THE TIDE'S TURN

The Tide's Turn

by

June Davies

Dales Large Print Books
Long Preston, North Yorkshire,
BD23 4ND, England.

British Library Cataloguing in Publication Data.

Davies, June
    The tide's turn.

    A catalogue record of this book is
    available from the British Library

    ISBN   978-1-84262-684-9 pbk

First published in Great Britain in 2008
by D.C. Thomson & Co. Ltd.

Published in Large Print 2009 by arrangement with
June Davies

Dales Large Print is an imprint of Library Magna Books Ltd.

Printed and bound in Great Britain by
T.J. (International) Ltd., Cornwall, PL28 8RW

An Absent Friend

Flames of autumnal sun were streaking the early morning sky as Charlotte Vale, striding along the deserted, shell-strewn beach below Hild Head, tightened the ribbons of her bonnet and drew her cloak closer about her against the keen off-shore wind.

The plaintive cries of the herring gulls that soared above the billowing grey tide echoed her own melancholy as she paused, raising her face to the wind, and stared out across the endless expanse of ocean.

Today was Andrew's twenty-first birthday and, in his last letter to her, he'd promised to be home for the occasion, but he hadn't come. Indeed, she'd heard nothing from him at all since before Easter.

Not that Andrew had ever had much patience for letter writing. Although she'd written to him faithfully every month since he'd gone away, his replies had been few – becoming ever fewer as the years had passed.

With a sigh, she looked back along the beach to watch the grey and white dog that was raising flurries of wet sand and seaweed at the water's edge, and reasoned for the thousandth time that Andrew must be very busy in America and would have more important things to do with his time than write to her.

After all, he had the excitements and adventures of living and working in a new world, of doing new things every day and meeting new people whereas, apart from helping Ma and Pa in the parish, what was there for Charlotte herself to do but write letters and wait?

'Snuffy! *Snuffy!*' she called to the mongrel collie who was now chasing skeins of blowing sand. 'This way– Hurry, or you'll get wet!'

Keeping just a yard or so clear of the advancing waves, Charlotte followed the ragged coastline. She'd been scarcely more than a child when Andrew Holcomb had sailed for South Carolina four years ago and she recalled how they'd spent that final day together here on the sands – herself, Andrew and Will Jervis.

They'd borrowed a boat and had rowed down to the smugglers' cove and while the boys had bathed, she'd paddled in the warm shallows. Then they'd roamed the empty beaches and scrambled on the cliffs, talking and laughing just as they had done every summer for as long as Charlotte could remember. Then, tired and hungry, the three friends had climbed up Caedmon's Trod to the ruined abbey and had eaten their picnic supper as the sun went down.

Night had fallen before the three trailed homewards along the cliff path.

They'd said their goodbyes at the lychgate of St Hild's church, and Charlotte had stood a moment, watching the figures of the two boys disappear into the shadows of the beach wood, as they headed inland towards the glimmering lights of the Holcombs' big house at Gaw Hill.

Then, with Snuffy at her heels, she'd fled back to the parsonage, scrubbing away her tears with the backs of her hands as she ran. Andrew was her dearest and best friend – and now he was gone!

But she was to see him once more before his ship sailed on the early tide.

It had been hours later, long past midnight and the quarter-moon had risen, its brilliant silvery light washing her low-ceilinged room under the eaves when the sound of tiny stones rattling down on to the wooden floor had wakened her. Andrew's deep voice was calling her name as she sat up and threw back the bedcovers.

In an instant, she was at the window and leaning out into the warm, still air.

'Andrew!' she whispered in amazement. 'I'll come down!'

'No need!' His white smile flashed into a broad grin. 'I'll come up!'

Charlotte's eyes had widened as he'd deftly vaulted on to the sloping slate roof of the scullery below her window, and shinned up the rough stone wall, sliding over the worn windowsill to her side.

'Andrew,' she whispered, suddenly slightly breathless. 'What are you doing here – and have you been *drinking?*'

'Ah, you find me out! I came here via the Old White Bear and a tankard of the landlord's finest ale! I ran all the way,' he went on, pushing a hand roughly through his hair. 'I'd soon had enough of Father and Hester's conversation tonight, so I slipped out of the house. Didn't want to wake Will by going anywhere near the stable for Caesar, so I came on foot. I had to see you just once more, Lottie. To say goodbye.'

'We've already said our goodbyes,' she replied sadly.

'My dear girl, Will and I might be as close as brothers, but there are certain things a chap can't say or do in the presence of another...' He gently smoothed a stray wisp of hair from her forehead, his fingers trailing the length of the heavy braid coiled down around her shoulder. '...and saying goodbye to a girl is one of them.'

'Don't go then!' she begged him. 'You only came back from Edinburgh a few weeks ago, and just the day before yesterday you were talking about the glorious summer we were all going to have together– Now, suddenly, you're sailing half a world away!'

'Circumstances change, Lottie,' he whispered, his eyes moving briefly from her. 'You wouldn't believe how suddenly. *Everything* can change in a single moment!'

'I don't understand.' She shook her head unhappily. 'It doesn't make any sense! Now you've finished studying, I thought you were to work for your father's company in Whitby. How can you do that if you're thousands of miles away?'

'Trust me, Lottie. This *is* for the best.'

Resting his hands upon her narrow shoulders, he smiled down into her eyes.

'As you well know, I've never had the slightest interest in sitting on a high stool in

11

Father's office, living and breathing the shipping trade! I've never wanted to go to sea as he did, either.' He laughed shortly, tugging the end of her braid. 'Not for me a life spent sailing the world's oceans, eating ghastly food while cooped up with a crowd of grimy, sweat-stained ruffians.'

She smiled in spite of herself. Captain Holcomb, Andrew's father, was an old sea dog through and through, but she couldn't imagine his son as a seaman.

'But if you went into the family business you wouldn't be a sailor, would you?' she reasoned. 'You'd be *here,* helping your father run the Holcomb Line!'

'Running the Holcomb Line? I have neither the desire nor the ability!' he returned briskly. 'Good heavens, even Hester is better at it than I'd be! Father is never done telling me how capable my dear sister is. How the old girl pitched right in and virtually ran the whole show for a few weeks while he was in his sick bed! She was going into Whitby every single day and handling things.'

He took a measured breath, then tilted Charlotte's chin and raised her forlorn face to his.

'Lottie, I'm not leaving Hild Head – or you – by choice. You do understand that,

12

don't you? But, until I'm twenty-one and come into money of my own, I have little choice but to do whatever Father wishes.'

She nodded, resigned. Nothing she could say would make any difference.

'Are you sailing on one of your father's ships?'

'Both are at sea and I needed…' he hesitated. 'Neither of Father's ships are due home for a while, but Hester found a clipper waiting to sail from Whitby for America – she pores over the shipping bulletins and reports like they're a map to the Holy Grail – and she managed to get me aboard. When we dock, I'll travel a short distance to the home of an old business friend of Father's. I'm to live with Mr Duchesney's family near Charleston and assist in his import and export company. You see, Father and Hester are determined to make me a man of commerce!'

He sighed deeply, cupping her heart-shaped face within his hands. 'My word, but you're a lovely one! You will wait for me, won't you? I couldn't bear to return from America and find you'd married some clod-hopping bore.'

'I'll wait for you, Andrew,' she vowed. 'I'll wait for you always!'

'Dear sweet Lottie! How I'll miss you!'

13

Drawing her closer, he brushed her forehead with a kiss.

'I must keep reminding myself how very young you are–'

'I've turned fifteen!' she protested. 'Lots of girls in Hild Head are wed before they're my age.'

'You have not the slightest idea of all you mean to me,' he murmured thickly, holding her a moment longer before moving away. 'Nor of what it costs me to leave you tonight!'

'Andrew–' she choked on his name, the stinging tears spilling unbidden from her eyes.

'Shhh. I can't stand tears. Look, I'd almost forgotten about this.'

From the folds of his white shirt he withdrew a single apricot rose, just beginning to ripen from bud to flower.

'I plucked it from the bush outside my window. Will you wear it on your bodice tomorrow, as a keepsake?'

She nodded, unable to speak.

'Good girl. Now, I must go.' Briefly embracing her once more, he moved across to the window.

'Wait! I'll let you out downstairs!'

'No, it's more fun this way.'

He was down at ground level in a trice.

14

'Don't forget me, sweet Lottie!' he called back up to her.

Forgetting Andrew was as impossible as forgetting to breathe. Not a single day had passed without Charlotte thinking of him, and missing him.

Now, four years later, as she wandered along the shoreline towards Jonas Rock, with Snuffy prancing and racing ahead of her, she wasn't able to quell the growing fear that, while she had never forgotten him, perhaps Andrew Holcomb had forgotten – and forsaken – *her*.

Rounding the gigantic jutting rock, Whitby slid into Charlotte's sight.

Morning sun burnished the ancient abbey's ruined walls and gleamed down upon the tiers of red-roofed dwellings which cast wells of deep shadow into the old town's steep, cobbled streets and narrow ghauts.

Yawls, cobles and brigs with furled sails lay at anchor in the busy harbour, and she immediately spotted the blue and white colours of the Holcomb Line's flag fluttering atop a schooner moored at the distant quayside.

'Snuffy!' she called, for Jonas Rock was as far as they ever went on their walks. 'This way – let's go home!'

The wind was even sharper walking back, and she quickened her pace until presently, the silhouette of St Hild's steeple appeared on the skyline and, hitching her skirts clear of the salt pools, she broke into a run, darting between the bands of deep water and crossed the hard sand ridges to the rough-hewn steps cut horizontally along the face of Hild Head cliffs.

The rock here was green and slippery, the climb steep and strenuous, and her cheeks were flushed from exertion when at last she hauled herself up the last step and emerged on to the narrow cliff path.

Snuffy was already sitting there patiently waiting, her plumy tail wagging.

'It's all right for you, you've got four–'

'Charlotte! Wait!'

Turning, she saw the Holcombs' heavily laden wagon trundling along the stony old drover's track.

'Want a ride?' Will Jervis grinned, jumping down and offering her his rough hand so she might clamber aboard. 'How about you, Snuffy? Or are you going to run all the way? No?'

Setting down the collie on the seat to one side of Charlotte, Will took his place on the other, lightly looping the reins through his fingers and quietly geeing the sturdy brown pony onwards toward St Hild's.

'I'm just up from the fish market,' he said, deftly guiding the wagon around a narrow curve that sheered away dangerously at the cliff edge. 'Miss Hester asked me to leave a box of fish at the parsonage.'

'It's very kind of Hester to always think of us. Do be sure to thank her, won't you?'

'I will, but you know what she's like – doesn't like to make a fuss about such things.'

'Nevertheless, we do appreciate her generosity.'

They'd jogged along for a while in a comfortable silence before Will asked. 'How are you today, Charlotte?'

'It being Andrew's birthday and him having broken his promise to be here with us?'

'Aye, summat like that.'

She studied the stony path directly ahead of them, finally giving voice to her fears. 'What if he never comes back?'

'He must,' Will answered in his blunt manner. 'For Master's not getting any younger, nor stronger, and the company can't run itself. If Andrew doesn't come home soon, he'll likely not have a company to come home to!'

17

'You haven't heard from him, then?' she persisted earnestly. 'He hasn't written to you?'

'Nay, Charlotte!' He laughed shortly. 'Andrew won't know that I can read and write now – nor would I be able to, if you hadn't taken the trouble to learn – to *teach* – me!'

'I only wish I'd done so sooner,' she responded in a small voice. She felt guilty about that. Not least because she'd suggested the weekly lessons at the parsonage chiefly to fill the void left by Andrew's departure. Will had been an eager, hard-working pupil, and Charlotte had quickly realised how much the skills of reading and writing meant to her old friend.

'It was thoughtless of me to leave it so long.'

'Ah, don't fret on it,' he replied easily, slowing the pony as they passed the church and approached the parsonage. 'There was never time when Andrew was here – he always wanted to be rushing off and about and doing things – you didn't have chance to sit teaching me my letters!'

She said nothing. He was absolutely right, of course.

'I've finished the Walter Scott novel your pa lent me,' he went on, helping her down

18

from the wagon. 'I struggled with it, but I took my time and ended up liking it.'

'It's one of Pa's favourites. He'll look forward to hearing what you think of it. Will you come to dinner on Sunday?'

'Aye, if I can get away from Gaw Hill. Thanks.'

Shouldering the box of fish, he followed her along the garden path and down the sea-facing side of the squat, stone parsonage.

'Pa's got the latest edition of *Bartlett's Magazine* for you, too.' Charlotte added, pushing open the kitchen door. 'Remind me to fetch it for you before you go.'

'I'll be clearing the last of the fruit from the orchard this morning,' he told her as he strode across the flagged scullery and set down the fish box on the cold marble shelf in the adjoining pantry. 'I'll bring some over later. Happen there'll be some taters and parsnips as well.'

Charlotte went out into the hallway, slipped off her bonnet and cloak and popped her head around the parlour door.

The Reverend and Mrs Vale were seated at the round table eating breakfast.

'I'm back!' she called, stepping aside as Snuffy darted past her into the warm, cheery room. 'And Will's with me – we met on the

19

cliff path.'

'Well don't leave the poor lad out there in the cold, bring him in for some breakfast!' chided Jacob Vale. 'Bessie's keeping the porridge hot.'

'I'll ask if he can stay– Oh, and Hester's sent us a box of fish!'

Turning from the parlour and closing the door behind her, Charlotte went back to the kitchen. Will was warming his hands before the glowing fire where the porridge pan gently simmered and the tea kettle bubbled up towards boiling.

'Can you stay for breakfast?'

He eyed the pot of creamy porridge hungrily and inhaled the tantalising smell of bread baking in the ovens on either side of the fire.

'I'd best not. Cook'll be waiting for the fish. And I've already dawdled a fair bit this morning–'

'If you'll not stay for breakfast,' chipped in Bessie Proud, bustling in with an armful of linen. 'At least take a cob of hot bread and some cheese with you.'

The plump housekeeper disappeared through to the wash house with the laundry before reappearing, tying a voluminous white apron about her middle as she went into the pantry for a round of strong, crumbly cheese.

'We'll not see a handsome young lad like you starve!'

'Thank you kindly, fair maid!' Will bowed grandly. 'I shall visit here again.'

'I'm more matron than maid, and I'm none too sure about the "fair" part, neither!' chuckled Bessie, bending to carefully take a tray of crusty brown baps from the oven. 'There's been no word from Andrew Holcomb, I take it?'

Charlotte shook her head, at once downcast. 'That's what Will and I have been talking about.'

'Never you mind, miss. There's no sense mithering about summat far away, especially when there's better on your own doorstep.' Cutting a thick wedge of cheese, Bessie set it down on to a clean cloth. 'Bread and cheese for your trouble, Will, and one of my fine strong onions for your cheek.'

'We three were all so happy together, Bessie!' mumbled Charlotte sadly. 'Why did Andrew have to go away and spoil everything!'

Bessie Proud finished wrapping the food and handed the parcel to Will, whose knowing gaze briefly met her own.

'I daresay it were all for the best, miss,' she murmured.

Worrying Times

The first frost of winter was sparkling on the fallen copper leaves that carpeted the wood as Charlotte wandered with her basket, seeking out evergreens or any attractive boughs bearing the last of the year's wild fruits. She already had some yew from the churchyard itself, and skeins of pretty ivy from the parsonage's garden wall, but what Charlotte really needed was something bright – red or orange fungi, perhaps – to deck the church gaily for Sally Poulsom's wedding that afternoon. Sally's father was landlord of The Old White Bear, so it was to be a lavish affair, with music and singers in the church and celebrations afterwards at the inn.

Adding some clusters of rowan berries, a sheaf of feathery, wheat-coloured reed grass from the stream's edge, and a few pink and cherry-red toadstools to her basket, Charlotte clambered over the stile and, with Snuffy at her heels, walked briskly through the north gate into the churchyard.

Humming cheerily, she pushed open the church's heavy door and strode inside, her boots clattering loudly as she started along the nave – freezing in her tracks when she spotted the woman who was on her knees before the window in the Lady Chapel.

'I'm so sorry, Hester!' she apologised, turning back to the doorway as the older woman looked up, startled from her devotions. 'I didn't mean to intrude.'

'You're not– I have no particular wish for solitude.' Hester Holcomb's quiet voice resonated in the silent church. 'Is the foliage for the Poulsom wedding?'

'Yes. I was lucky to find such a nice selection.'

'I understand Sally's husband-to-be is giving up his drayman's job in Whitby to work at The Bear– It'll be a real family concern then,' remarked Hester, who never missed a whit of local news. 'Sally's a nice girl. I hope she'll be very happy.'

While Miss Holcomb returned to her prayers, Charlotte softly proceeded across the aisle and began trimming the altar, as well as the ledges of the arched windows and the pew ends with the greenery, berries and fungi.

She could have kicked herself for blundering in on Hester's private remembrance of her mother! The Holcombs had dedicated the stained glass window of The Good Shepherd to Martha's memory and, if Charlotte had only thought, she'd have realised Hester would be there alone in prayer this morning, just as she was every year on the anniversary of her mother's death.

She deliberately did not glance in Hester's direction again, but quietly got on with her decorating.

She was just finishing, bending to tidy bits and bobs of stem and leaf into her basket, when she heard Hester's firm footsteps as she rose and moved about the church, then the quiet chink of heavy coins sliding into the parish poor box and the rustle of skirts as the older woman approached her.

'The church looks beautiful, Charlotte. Sally will be pleased.'

'I hope so.' Charlotte straightened up, hooking the basket over her arm. 'At least it's a dry day. I always think it's such a shame when it's raining and the bride gets a drenching in her finery!'

'Yes, indeed.' Hester fell into step beside her as Charlotte started towards the doorway. 'We're most fortunate to have such clement weather so late in the year. Why, the

Winter Fayre is almost upon us, and Christmas not far behind!'

'Pa was saying it'd be nice if we could hold a concert of sacred music at St Hild's during Advent – and even better if we could get Mr Rowbourne from Whitby to sing for us.'

'Edmund Rowbourne certainly has a splendid tenor voice,' agreed Hester thoughtfully. 'Perhaps he could be persuaded to donate his services for free for the occasion and then all the concert proceeds would benefit the needy of the parish. I'll write to him, and see what can be done.'

As they quit the church, both women glanced back along the nave.

Brilliant winter sunshine beamed through the tall windows of coloured glass to cast a kaleidoscope of deepest blue, red, green and gold across the worn stone floor.

'It looks so beautiful and peaceful, doesn't it?' murmured Charlotte. 'Whenever I see St Hild's like this, I always think of all the folk who've worshipped here these past 700 or so years, just as we do today.'

Hester nodded, then turned away and stepped outside.

'Andrew should be here, you know.' Her voice was sharp. 'Have *you* heard from him, Charlotte?'

Charlotte hesitated. She was reluctant to confide in Hester, aware that Andrew had never been close to his older sister.

'Not recently.'

'Doesn't surprise me.' Hester's reply was curt. 'He flaunts his lack of respect and family duty, but it's his utter disregard for Father that I will never forgive. If he possessed an iota of backbone or character, Andrew would feel thoroughly ashamed of himself but, knowing my brother as I do, I doubt if his conscience even pricks!'

Charlotte bridled. 'It wasn't Andrew's choice to go to America, Hester!' she snapped. 'Far from it; Andrew merely did as he was bidden – bidden by his family, I may remind you! – and was stalwart enough to decide to make the best of a decision not of his choosing. I'd say that shows a great deal of backbone and character!'

'You give my brother undeserved credit, child,' returned Hester tartly. 'Andrew has never done anything in his entire life that he didn't wish to do, or that wasn't for his own personal benefit. Perhaps part of the blame falls at my feet, for I brought him up, but I certainly did not raise him to be the irresponsible and selfish young man he has become!'

'Andrew is not selfish, nor irresponsible!

26

How can you say such dreadful things?' railed Charlotte, facing the prim woman angrily. 'Andrew is the most generous, caring–'

'Then why has he not written to any of us?' demanded Hester impatiently. 'When I – when Father and I – sent for him to come home a long while past, why did Andrew choose to ignore the instruction and stay away?'

'Well... Well, perhaps you shouldn't have sent him away in the first place!' retaliated Charlotte. 'He was happy here in Hild Head. Andrew didn't want to go to America but *you* arranged his passage and sent him there!'

'If my brother was half the man you believe him to be, the need for him to leave Hild Head and Whitby would never have arisen and–' Hester broke off, her pale lips pressed together. Adjusting the buttons on her gloves, she continued crisply, 'I would be obliged if Reverend and Mrs Vale and yourself would join Father and I for luncheon. Next Wednesday, if that would be convenient. Good day, Charlotte.'

With that, Hester turned on her heel and walked away stiff-backed through the churchyard, between the rows of weathered, and mostly humble, stone markers towards

27

the Holcomb family grave, where Martha Holcomb and her seven children who had not survived infancy lay at rest.

Despite the occasion and the surroundings, Charlotte was seething! How dare Hester be so self-righteous and domineering! Small wonder Andrew loathed her– 'Oh!' she cried, marching into the parsonage hallway and all but colliding with her father. 'Sorry, Pa!'

'My word, you've a face like a thunder-cloud, child!' Jacob Vale exclaimed mildly, winding an enormous muffler about his neck. 'What or whom has ruffled *your* feathers?'

'Hester Holcomb, the old witch!' muttered Charlotte, noisily kicking off her boots. 'She was saying the most horrible, spiteful, un-truthful things about Andrew!'

'Oh, Hester has a sharp tongue, that's for certain,' remarked Reverend Vale, jamming his shovel hat close upon his head to keep his ears warm. 'But I doubt the poor woman's ever held a broomstick, let alone sat astride one! And I daresay none of us are quite perfect.' His eyes twinkled over the rims of his silver spectacles at Charlotte. 'Are we now?'

She said nothing at first, tossing her cloak over the banister and banging her bonnet down on top of it. 'You didn't hear what she said about him, Pa. Nor the ... *vehemence* ... in the way she said it!'

Jacob sighed, buttoning up his coat. 'I'm going over to Ghyll Croft. Widow Tunstall's rheumatics are laying her low again. I'll be back in plenty of time for the wedding. Why don't you get yourself into the parlour, have a nice cup of tea, and help your ma with the quilt she's making for Lucy's baby? Four hands will get it finished a lot quicker than two!'

Edith Vale had overheard something of the commotion out in the hall and so wasn't surprised when her youngest daughter trailed into the parlour and flopped despondently into the rocking chair across the hearth from her.

Although the heat of her anger was dissipating, the altercation with Hester Holcomb still rankled and Charlotte felt edgy and troubled. Hester's revelation that Andrew hadn't returned to Hild Head even though he'd been summoned home by his family had shaken her.

'It's *her* fault he didn't come home,' she

29

mumbled at last, absently taking up her needlework. 'Andrew always said how horrible she was to him, but I never guessed she despised him so!'

Edith Vale looked up sharply. 'Whatever are you talking about?'

'The vicious things Hester was saying, Ma. She must really hate Andrew.'

'You're quite wrong about that, pet,' said Edith quietly. 'Hester's devoted to that boy. Family means everything to her.'

Charlotte shook her head. 'No, Ma. Andrew was absolutely right. He said Hester was a miserable old maid, the wrong side of thirty-five and sour as crab apples – and she is!'

'I'm surprised at Andrew's heartlessness,' Edith commented, passing the box of patchworks to Charlotte. 'It was cruel of him to describe his sister in such terms.'

'But it's true, Ma!' protested Charlotte, starting her corner of the quilt. 'Hester used always to be nagging and telling him what to do. She never liked to see him happy or having any fun!'

'I don't think that's true, do you?' queried Charlotte's mother gently. 'Hester *is* strict, but she only ever wanted the very best for Andrew. The Holcombs weren't always well-doing, you know. Samuel worked hard as the master of other people's ships for many years before he saved enough to buy one of his own.

'After Hester was born, her mother, Martha, lost a lot of other babies and, although the doctors warned her against any more children, Martha never gave up hope because she knew how badly Samuel wanted a son.'

'Then Andrew was born,' said Charlotte uneasily, in her mind's eye seeing Hester once more bowed in prayer at the Lady Chapel. 'And Mrs Holcomb died.'

'Hester was only a girl, as pretty and lively as any you ever saw,' Edith Vale continued. 'But on that day she had to grow up. I daresay she dreamed of dances and socials, as young girls do. Probably she'd hoped for marriage and children, too. Instead, she set all that aside and devoted her whole life to caring for her grieving father, bringing up Andrew, and becoming mistress of Gaw Hill herself.'

'I'd never thought about Hester being young,' murmured Charlotte, her eyes upon her sewing. 'Nor of what it must really have been like for her to lose her mother.'

Edith leaned across, squeezing her

daughter's hand. 'Next time Hester's prickly manner vexes you, love, try to remember all she willingly gave up for Andrew and her father. The years have flown now, her youth and prospects of marriage are gone. What is there stretching before Hester but long years of lonely spinsterhood?'

'I must apologise again for Father not joining us for luncheon,' Hester Holcomb was saying the following Wednesday, while she and the Vales were seated around the table. 'I know he was looking forward to it very much.'

'Some matter of business has cropped up to detain him, I expect.'

'It invariably does, Edith,' a frown creased Hester's forehead. 'Father works far too hard. I've tried to persuade him to pass more of the business matters on to Jenkins. He's been Father's clerk for the last twenty-odd years and is utterly trustworthy. Provided he's given clear instructions, the man is perfectly capable– But Father pays me no heed.'

'Ah, Samuel's as stubborn as a mule, Hester. And he's missed a fine meal today and no mistake!' commented Reverend Vale. 'I'd hoped he and I could've set the world to rights while we ate, but I suppose we'll have to wait until our next chess night to solve all the nation's problems!'

Hester laughed, and Charlotte was taken aback at how different she looked when her face was lively and animated. 'There's naught Father likes better than a good argument!'

'No, no, Hester– Not *argument,* civilised rhetoric and discussion! The sort of thing Socrates and Aristotle and them sort of fellers went in for.'

'Jacob, I've overheard some of your discussions with my father, and I don't recall them ever sounding like the Ancient Greeks!'

'Ancient fishwives, more like!' chipped in Edith Vale. 'And folk say it's women who can talk till the cows come home!'

'Er, Hester,' said the Reverend, beaming. 'Is there a drop more in the pot, by any chance?'

'You wouldn't be changing the subject?' asked Charlotte, passing along his cup. 'Would you, Pa?'

'We-ll, I just might!'

'Guest's privilege.' Hester smiled as she poured the tea. 'Would anyone like more cake? Or fruit? There's–'

Her words were drowned out by the ringing of rapid hoof beats upon the drive, followed by the crashing of the knocker against the great oak front door.

Hester was already on her feet and crossing the dining-room when the little maid, Liddie, burst inside.

'It's Master – he's been taken badly!'

Sweeping past her, Hester strode out to the scarlet-faced lad who was hovering on the doorstep.

'What exactly has happened to Captain Holcomb?' she demanded.

'Dunno, missus.' He sniffed. 'I were just told to come with the message.'

'Is he still alive?' she persisted harshly. 'You must know if he's alive or dead, boy!'

'Don't, missus…' He screwed up his face. 'All I know is that the doctor's been sent for.'

'Is the Captain at his offices? At Crown Buildings?'

'Aye, missus. That's where Mr Jenkins sent me from.'

Hester turned her attention to the maid. 'Find Will. Tell him what's happened and to bring round the carriage. I must get to town as speedily as possible.' She was already starting up the stair. 'Oh, and Liddie, see to the boy!'

Shocked and alarmed, the Vales had been standing stock-still in the dining-room

34

doorway. Now Charlotte darted after their hostess, catching hold of her arm. 'I'll come with you!'

Within ten minutes, their anxious journey was underway.

Will manoeuvred the carriage skilfully and at speed away from Gaw Hill, through Hild Head village, past The Old White Bear and on to the steep, winding track down into the old town.

Clattering across the bridge and past the town hall, he steered sharply away from the prosperous streets with their elegant shops and coffee houses and headed along to the waterfront, weaving through the jostling traffic crowding the wharf and around to the dark, towering frontage of Crown Buildings, where the Holcomb Line had its chambers.

Charlotte had not known what to say to comfort Hester, and so they had travelled in silence.

Now, as the older woman hastily alighted from the carriage, she glanced sidelong at her companion. 'I hope Father is still alive, Charlotte. I pray he has not died without family near!'

Charlotte echoed that prayer as she followed Hester up the stairs and along a labyrinth of tiled corridors, before hurrying across a small outer office past a cluster of onlookers and finally into a larger room beyond.

There, several tall, middle-aged men stood talking quietly, gathered around the black leather couch where Samuel Holcomb lay pale and still.

Pushing between them, Hester was at once at her father's side.

Taking one of his hands in both of her own, she looked up fearfully into the face of a red-haired man wearing spectacles.

'He's still alive – but only just,' Dr Hawkes said unemotionally. 'It was an extremely severe attack this time, much worse than anything he's had before. I've given him something to ease the pain, and to make him sleep.'

'Can he be moved, Dr Hawkes?'

'Providing care and time are taken on the journey. He'll not waken for at least six hours.'

'Shall I go downstairs and tell Will?' suggested Charlotte quietly. 'So he might make the arrangements?'

'Tell your man a stretcher will be required.' It was the physician who replied, scribbling on a notepad and tearing off several leaves.

'Give him this – it has the instructions he'll need. And he's also to collect these items from the apothecary. Oh, and tell him he's to do these errands immediately – there's to be no idling or time-wasting,' added the doctor, as Charlotte sped from the office.

'Dr Hawkes suggested I should engage a nurse,' confided Hester, when at last they were on their way back to Gaw Hill. 'But I refused. I shall care for Father myself. I've done it before, so I've an idea what to expect.'

'I'm sure he'd much rather be looked after by you than by a stranger,' agreed Charlotte.

The doctor was accompanying them on horseback. The journey was of necessity made at a moderate pace and a moonless night had fallen as the carriage bearing Charlotte and Hester led a sombre little procession up and away from the old town. The darkness was impenetrable, and Charlotte had long since lost any inkling of their bearings.

'I don't know how Will sees to drive so surely on a night such as this.'

'Will's a good man. He has many skills,' remarked Hester, flexing her stiff shoulders. 'He's honest and loyal, and has a good head as well as a good heart. He could rise in this world and make a secure future for himself in the town – or anywhere – but I'm sure he'll never wish to leave Gaw Hill.'

'Why not?' queried Charlotte. She'd never actually thought about Will leaving the Holcombs, but neither had she thought about him remaining their hired man for the rest of his life.

Hester didn't answer immediately. 'I rather think Will has his own reasons, Charlotte. Reasons powerful enough to make him bide.'

The flaring torches outside The Old White Bear lit their way through the village, then they were plunged once again into total blackness for two or three miles more until the lights of the Holcombs' square, substantial Georgian house began to glimmer through the trees.

'I shall stay tonight– That's if you wish me to, of course.'

'It's kind of you, Charlotte. I'm sure it won't be necessary for you to stay all night, but,' Hester hesitated awkwardly. 'But I *would* be grateful if you could stay a little while? Just until Father is settled and Dr Hawkes has attended to him. Once he is made comfortable and is sleeping peacefully in his own bed, I shan't feel quite so … afraid.'

Impulsively, Charlotte reached across in the darkness and tightly gripped the other woman's gloved hand.

'Hester, if there's anything – anything at all – that my parents or I can do to help while Captain Holcomb is poorly, you must tell us at once! What else are friends and neighbours for?'

Charlotte could see Hester's face only dimly as they approached the house, but it was sufficient a glimpse to reveal the wetness of tears on the older woman's cheek.

'Poor Father! He's worked so hard all his life, and now that he's getting old and ill, running the company is just too much for him!'

'Perhaps he might retire?' ventured Charlotte vaguely.

'If only! But how can he?' cried Hester, her words emotional and ragged. 'He is determined the Holcomb Line be prosperous and flourishing when he passes it on to Andrew so that he in turn might pass it on to *his* sons! It's going to be Andrew's company one day, Charlotte. He should be here now! Instead, he left Charleston without a word to anybody and was last seen somewhere in New Orleans!'

Hester's hand rested on the door of the

carriage as it drew to a halt before the steps of Gaw Hill.

'I just can't stop thinking that if Andrew had come home two years ago when he was first sent for, then Father would not be lying nearer to death than life this night!'

It was considerably later that evening when Dr Hawkes rode from Gaw Hill, leaving behind medicinal preparations and meticulous instructions.

'He's to visit again on the morrow,' Hester whispered, when Charlotte looked in to bid her goodnight. 'I shall sit with Father tonight. Just in case.'

She was seated at Captain Holcomb's bedside, although he was still sleeping deeply and was insensible of her presence.

'Shouldn't you get some rest, Hester? You look exhausted.'

'I'm all right.' She smiled. 'Thank you for staying with me, Charlotte. Goodnight.'

'Goodnight, Hester.'

Moving soundlessly from Captain Holcomb's room, Charlotte descended the wide staircase and waited in the hallway while Liddie fetched her bonnet and cloak.

'Here we are, miss! I'll just get Will to bring the carriage around!'

'No, don't do that, Liddie. I'll see to it.'

'Night then, miss,' said the little maid, shutting the great front door.

For a moment, Charlotte stood on the steps gazing up at the window of the dimly-lit room where Hester kept her lonely vigil at Captain Holcomb's bedside.

Then, all of a sudden, she wanted to be at home with her mother and father as quickly as possible and she sped around the side of the house. Even as her light footsteps pattered on the cobbled yard, she spied a dull glow appearing in Will's room above the stables as he struck light to a lantern and shinned down the ladder to her side.

'How's Master?'

'The same. Hester's sitting with him.'

He nodded. 'I'll get the wagon–'

'I'd rather walk, Will. If you don't mind?'

He fell into step beside her, and as they entered the beech wood, he cast a backward glance towards the house.

'I don't like thinking of her in that big old house, with Lord only knows what worries and fears going round inside her head.'

'The doctors said that given time Captain Holcomb should recover, Will.'

'Happen, but he'll never be the man he was. Not after this. And Hester knows it.

41

She's a good head on her shoulders. She'll be fretting for the family's future.'

Charlotte's brow creased. 'The company *did* seem to be preying on her mind.'

'As well it might!' he retorted. 'Hester and the Captain have the same salt blood in their veins. They both love the sea and shipping and that blessed company! If only Miss Hester were a man, then the Holcomb Line would be set fair for a bright future. As it is, everything depends on Andrew coming home and pulling his weight– It'll not survive otherwise!'

They walked a while without conversation, the beech wood filled with the sound of small footfalls amongst dry leaves, as countless scurrying, snuffling little animals went about their business.

'You really are very fond of Hester, aren't you?' Charlotte remarked at length.

'Does that surprise you?' Will glanced down at her. 'Hester's a fine woman. She's what's held Gaw Hill together all these years. And she it was who took me in when I was left a foundling at St Hild's.

'The Holcombs have given me home, work and a place to belong – but don't run away with the notion I'm just beholden. It runs much deeper than that, Charlotte. The Captain and Miss Hester are all the family I've ever known, and I care for them *as* family!'

Charlotte nodded, recollecting Hester's saying Will had good reason to bide at Gaw Hill. Then something else Hester Holcomb had said – or rather implied – came rushing into her mind.

'Will, was Andrew in some sort of trouble when he went to America? Is that why he had to go away so suddenly?'

Will didn't answer, and Charlotte caught at his arm so he might face her. 'I'm a child no longer. Tell me!'

He shrugged, looking away from her and towards where the shore and the sea lay concealed in the blackness of the moonless winter night. 'You recall Andrew's high spirits when he came home from Edinburgh that summer?'

'Of course! He was celebrating finishing his studies– We had such fine jaunts, the three of us!'

'Aye, well, happen when you and me weren't with him, Andrew went off on a few jaunts of his own,' said Will carefully. 'He took to drinking a bit too much and fell in with some ne'er-do-wells in Whitby. I reckon the Holcombs didn't think it fitting for a gentleman to be mixed up with such a rough crowd.'

'I see.' Charlotte chewed her lip, pausing as they reached the parsonage gate.

The suddenness of Andrew's departure and his reluctance to explain the reason for it, made perfect sense now. He would have been embarrassed and ashamed to admit to such foolishness.

'So the Captain sent Andrew away to keep him out of harm's way.'

'You'd best get indoors, Charlotte.' Will reached across to the gate, stepping aside so she might enter ahead of him. 'You'll catch cold, standing out here.'

'Won't you come in for a hot drink?' She opened the door softly, mindful that the household were in bed. 'Bessie will have left something out.'

'Nay. I'll get back. If Master or Miss Hester need me, I want to be close by.'

'Of course– Oh, Will!' she whispered urgently as he turned to leave. 'There was something else Hester said today – about sending for Andrew to come home two years ago, but he ignored her. And now he's gone off on his own to New Orleans! Is it so?' She searched his face earnestly. 'Is it? Has he been in touch with you? Why did you not tell me, Will? How could you *not* tell me?'

'Calm yourself, Charlotte! I've heard nothing from Andrew since he sailed for America. Nor have I been told of where he is or what he's doing.'

His voice was harsh, an uncharacteristic flash of anger brightening his eyes as he glowered down at her. 'Whatever *I* may think of *them*, the Holcombs do not confide their family affairs to me – to them, I'm just their hired hand, remember!'

'My, you're looking comely! Could be you're the prettiest wench at the Winter Fayre,' declared Will a month later, sidling up alongside Charlotte as she browsed a stall selling ribbons and buttons. 'Mind, I've only just brought the Holcombs down from Gaw Hill, so I've not had time to eye up the rest of the girls yet!'

'Cheek!' She swiped at him with her mittens. 'How is Captain Holcomb?'

'Pleased to be out of the house at long last! Miss Hester wasn't keen on bringing him out for the first time on such a bitter cold day, but Master kicked up a fuss – said he hadn't missed a Winter Fayre since he came ashore for good; twenty-odd years ago! In the end, Miss Hester had to give in and said he could come down for a few hours!'

Charlotte had glimpsed the little party from Gaw Hill arriving in the village a short while earlier, with Captain Holcomb swathed in blankets and being pushed in a wheeled chair.

'Ma and Pa and I visited Hester and the Captain last week. He seems so much *smaller*, somehow. He was always such a robust man.'

'Still is– In voice and bluster, at least!'

'Hester was saying there hasn't been any news of Andrew, yet?' she ventured quietly.

'Nay. Miss Hester's at her wits' end keeping the company to rights. Every day I go into the office to do a few jobs and collect books and papers and such, and whenever Master doesn't need her, Miss Hester works on them with me and writes down Mr Jenkins' duties for the next day. Come morning, I take the lot back into town and bring a fresh bundle home. It can't go on, though,' he concluded sombrely. 'Soon as Captain Holcomb's strong enough, he'll have to decide what's to be done with the Holcomb Line.'

'The clerk – Mr Jenkins – has been employed there for ever,' remarked Charlotte as they weaved through the noisy, jostling crowd towards a troupe of gaily-attired tumblers. 'Couldn't he run the company for them?'

'Maybe,' considered Will, steering Char-

46

lotte and Snuffy safely past the fire-eater's billowing flames. 'It's not the same, though, is it? He's not family and the Holcomb Line is a family concern. Having an outsider in charge of it wouldn't sit comfortably with Captain Holcomb. Nor with Miss Hester, either, come to that.'

With Charlotte at his side, Will stood surveying the Fayre, still busy and bustling despite the fading daylight. Lanterns were starting to be lit, and there was already a flurry of activity beyond The Old White Bear at the tithe barn, where the night's dancing was to take place.

'I'd best get across to the inn. I left the Captain there with a mug of ale and his cronies, while Miss Hester looked around the stalls. We arranged to meet up again before dusk. She wants him home before full dark.'

'Aren't you staying for the dancing?' exclaimed Charlotte in dismay.

'I'll get back here as soon as I can,' he answered, glancing towards the tithe barn where torches were being fixed outside the huge doors, and a platform was being put together for the musicians. 'If I'm lucky, I might even get a dance with the prettiest girl at the Fayre!'

Charlotte beamed up at him, her cheeks

rosy and warm with more than the afternoon's chill air. 'Don't be too long. Ma and Pa won't be staying late!'

That dark, wintry night, the tithe barn was ringing with music, laughter and dancing feet.

Two fiddlers, a bell-ringer, a penny-whistler, a fat man with a concertina and a tall lanky fellow blowing a flute played lively tunes for the dancers who were tripping and whirling about the barn's earthen floor.

Will and Charlotte stood watching from the sidelines, tapping their toes and clapping their hands in time to the infectious rhythms.

Covered jack-o-lanterns glowed on the trestle tables where sellers were doing a brisk trade in roasted chestnuts, oranges, pies and sweetmeats.

The Poulsom family from The Bear were kept busy replenishing tankards of ale and cider for the men, while for the womenfolk there was spiced fruit punch or cordial.

'Your pa and ma look a treat dancing together!' commented Will, bending close to Charlotte's ear to make himself heard.

She smiled a little wistfully. Her parents, as if unaware of the breathless reels and gallops being attempted by their fellows, were gliding and dipping in the fashion of some old, favourite dance from their youth.

Quite unexpectedly, Charlotte felt a sharp pang of deep loneliness.

'I hope I'll be as happy as Ma and Pa,' she said, raising sad eyes to him. 'To love and to be loved in return is all that really matters, isn't it?'

'Aye, it is.' His expression softened as he looked down into the heart-shaped face so close to his own. 'Being rich counts for nowt without somebody to share it.'

For a long moment, the lantern light, the music, the laughter and the dancers who were swirling around them in a blur of sounds and colours seemed far away.

Wordlessly, Will took Charlotte into his arms. 'Can I have a dance,' he murmured, holding her close, 'with the prettiest girl at the Fayre?'

Charlotte couldn't speak, but her sparkling eyes gave answer and he proudly led her out into the throng. Gazing up at him as they swirled and swayed and moved together in time to the sweeping, soaring music, she couldn't believe she was dancing like this – feeling like this. Her heart was thumping, her senses racing, her thoughts spinning and she didn't notice a curious murmur stirring through the noisy, crowded barn.

'May I cut in?' The deep voice with the slightest trace of American accent was very, very close behind Charlotte, 'and exercise the prerogative of the prodigal son by claiming this dance?'

Return Of The Prodigal Son

'Andrew–!' Spinning around at the sound of his voice, Charlotte all but stepped straight into his waiting arms and before she could recover herself, he'd seized the moment, sweeping her from Will upon the rhythmic swell of music.

Craning her neck, she caught but a glimpse of Will before being borne away into the dance. Feeling the warmth of Andrew's breath against her cheek, she turned to look up at him and drew breath to speak, but words would not come. In a sudden rush of emotion, she felt the prickle of tears and at once lowered her lashes, hot colour rising to her cheeks.

He bent closer, speaking into her ear. 'Aren't you going to say you're pleased to see me, Lottie?'

Raising her eyes, she saw that he was laughing and she immediately relaxed into the curve of his arms, finding her voice at last.

'I can't believe you're really here!'

51

The tune was ending but he didn't relinquish his hold on her, maintaining it for a few moments after the notes faded before reluctantly releasing her and leading her towards the barn's wide doors.

'We can't leave!' she protested. 'What about Will? And Ma and Pa?'

'There are so many people cavorting in here that your parents won't even miss you,' he returned. 'And as for Will... I don't want to share these first precious moments with anyone! Besides, we aren't leaving. Just going somewhere quieter.'

After the heat and gaiety of the tithe barn, the frosty night was cold and still and Charlotte shivered.

Andrew at once took off his cloak. 'Wrap this around you.' He pulled the thick warmth of the garment snugly about her shoulders. 'Better?'

'Mmm. Isn't it a beautiful night?' She sighed, snuggling deeper into the warmth and gazed up at the starry sky. 'It's as though there's only you and I in the whole world!'

'Apart from the scores just a few yards away in the barn, you mean?' he grinned, adding, 'I didn't see Father or Hester inside, and they've never been known to miss the

Winter Fayre.'

'They were here earlier, but Will drove them home before dusk–' She broke off. 'Your father's been very ill, Andrew. Didn't you know?'

'No, I didn't,' he replied simply. 'How is he now?'

'Much recovered, but still very poorly. Will wrote to you straight away.'

'Will did?' he echoed. 'I didn't realise he could write! Anyhow, I didn't receive any letter. And Father's on the mend, you say?'

'He uses a chair with wheels now, but he's much improved. It was very serious. Hester feared he might not survive. We all did. Will's been helping her run the Holcomb Line.'

'Has he indeed?' He suddenly shuddered, resting an arm across Charlotte's shoulders and moving away from the barn and across The Old White Bear's cobbled yard. *'I'm feeling cold now – too many balmy Southern nights, I expect!'*

Approaching a carriage standing against a sheltered wall, he opened the door and offered Charlotte his hand.

'We can't just get into someone else's carriage without permission!'

'We're merely seeking shelter from the bitter winter night.' He grinned, bundling her inside. 'It's not as though we intend driving off in the thing – since there isn't a horse at the front end, we wouldn't get very far!'

Charlotte laughed, settling into the deep, comfortable upholstery.

Andrew had a way of making everything seem happy and carefree and perfect.

'Isn't this better?' He closed the carriage door with a solid click.

The cold of the night and the music, laughter and voices of the Winter Fayre were shut out, and the warmth and intimacy of the velvet-lined carriage enveloped them.

'There were times when I thought I'd never see Hild Head again. There were times when I never *wished* to – and others when my heart ached for all I'd left behind.'

'Was it awful?'

With only the flickering torches across the yard for light, Charlotte could not see his face clearly nor read the expression in his eyes.

'You never said much about it in your letters.'

'It was mostly a very good life, actually. I like America. There's an excitement, a sense of spirit and adventure, as though anything is possible!' He placed his arm about her shoulders and rested his cheek upon the softness of her hair. 'I felt as though the entire world was at my feet!'

'You sound as though you enjoyed it,' she murmured, somehow disappointed that he had not pined for her as she had for him. 'Tell me about where you lived and what you did.'

'Well, the Duchesneys have a huge estate – a plantation they call it – near Charleston. Their house is enormous, four times the size of Gaw Hill, and life there is genteel and taken at a leisurely pace.

'Guy Duchesney – Father's old friend – is an extremely powerful and wealthy man. Living with his family taught me a great deal. One of the most valuable lessons being the importance of land,' concluded Andrew. 'Father has a couple of ships and the office in Whitby, but it's *land* that matters.'

'Are–' she began hesitantly, her heart thumping. 'Are you home for ever?'

'Forever is a very long time, Lottie.' He dropped his lips lightly to her forehead. 'Now, we've done nothing but talk about me; I want to hear what you've been up to.'

'Nothing's changed. It never does here, does it?' She considered. 'Oh, Lucy is married now. To a man called James Went-worth – you don't know him – he's an engineer and he works for a quarry up in the Lakes. They have a little girl called Bea. She's nearly two.'

'I'll wager that you make a sterling aunt!'

'I don't get the chance to be!' She grimaced. 'They live too far away. And there's to be another baby next year. Around Easter, I think.'

'What about suitors, Lottie?' he whispered against her hair, drawing her ever closer. 'Will I need to fight off a band of lusty swains—'

'Ah! This is where you've got to!'

The carriage door swung open and a blast of icy night air flooded inside.

And there stood Will Jervis, his hand outstretched. 'We'd best get back inside, Charlotte. Your ma and pa'll be wondering about you.'

'Oh, yes – I suppose so,' she responded ruefully, accepting his hand and clambering from the carriage.

She cast a glance over her shoulder at Andrew.

'I could come back and stay a while longer, once I've seen them and explained.'

But Andrew seemed not to hear her. He stepped from the carriage and she saw his attention was focussed upon Will as the boyhood friends faced each other. For a moment, neither spoke, and she felt a frisson of tension in the still air before Will's weather-browned face broke into a broad smile and he offered his hand to his old friend, using the other to clap him upon the shoulder.

'Welcome home – it's grand to see you!'

'You too, Will, old boy!' returned Andrew, grasping the offered hand and surveying the tall, squarely-set man standing before him. 'How's life been treating you?'

'Not so bad.' Will's eyes crinkled at the corners as he grinned. 'Been spending a bit too much time indoors of late, but I can't complain. You know about the Master, I take it?'

'Charlotte's been telling me,' Andrew answered soberly. 'I'd best get up to Gaw Hill, now. I saw Caesar in The Bear's stables. Did you ride him down here. He looks well. You've taken fine care of him, Will.'

'I take care of them all – no favourites!'

'I always could rely on you!' Andrew paused. 'I've stowed my luggage at The Bear and I'll ride Caesar home. You're all right for making your own way back, aren't you?'

While Will was saddling and fetching the horse, Andrew and Charlotte waited in The

Old White Bear's yard.

'Oh, Lottie,' he murmured, drawing her hand to his lips. 'Until I saw you dancing with Will tonight, I hadn't realised how desperately I've missed you!'

Charlotte couldn't answer. Vaguely aware of approaching hoofs on the icy cobbles, she slipped the cloak from her shoulders, instantly feeling cold and bereft. Andrew turned to Will, taking the reins.

'I'll see you in the morning, Will.' He shook his old friend's hand once more. 'We've a deal of catching up to do!'

'Aye, we have that.'

Leaning down from the saddle, Andrew tenderly touched Charlotte's upturned face. 'Goodnight, dearest Lottie – sleep well!'

Then, touching Caesar into a canter, he was gone into the winter's night.

Snuffy's claws scratching and clicking upon the smooth oaken floor, and her excited whining as she jumped up and down at the window ledge, awakened Charlotte next morning.

Stirring, she blinked open heavy eyes. The hour was late. She'd overslept. Stretching out under the covers, she allowed her eyes to close again. There were voices down below on the path, and with a start she was wide awake.

Perhaps Andrew had come to visit her – and she wasn't up, much less ready to receive him!

Scrambling from bed in a trice, and standing back from the window so that she couldn't be seen, she peered out sidelong – and saw the Gaw Hill wagon.

The visitor must be Will.

With a sigh, she sank down on to the edge of the bed, rubbing her sleepy eyes. She should've realised it was Will from Snuffy's delight. It was he who'd rescued the collie from drowning as a tiny pup and she'd always been devoted to him – he came second only to Charlotte in her affections.

Letting the dog out on to the landing so that she might race down and greet him, Charlotte dressed hastily.

Her parents were both in the hallway and beyond them, she could see that Will was carefully lifting a heavy, well-wrapped object from the wagon.

''Morning, Charlotte!' He smiled, manoeuvring the bulky item through the cottage's narrow front door and sharply around into Reverend Vale's study. 'I've put a new leg on, vicar, and I went round the edge and fixed the beading, too. It was coming a bit loose here and there.'

'That's fine workmanship!' responded Jacob, stooping stiffly to run his hands over the chess table as Will unwrapped the protective sacking. 'You've done a grand job. Just grand. Did I ever tell you my father taught me to play chess on this very table, just as *his* father had taught him and–'

'I think you might have mentioned it once or twice, Jacob,' chipped in Edith. 'If you don't have to rush away, Will, won't you have breakfast with us? After last night's festivities, we were all a bit late rising so we haven't eaten yet.'

'*Some* of us were even later than others,' put in Jacob, glancing at Charlotte over his spectacles before returning his attention to Will. 'And you won't risk mortally offending Bessie by refusing a dish of her porridge again, will you?'

'I'm not that reckless, vicar! Besides, it'll set me up for the day. As you can see,' Will indicated what he described as his 'town-going' clothes, 'I'm off into Whitby this morning, so if anyone needs anything doing, just give me a list.'

Reverend Vale shook his head. 'I've to go myself in a week or so, and I don't need anything that won't wait until then. How about you, Edith?'

'I don't think so – oh, Lucy's letter!' she recalled. 'I've made up a little parcel, with a new dress for Bea and some books for Lucy and James. Could you send those please, Will? If you're sure it's no bother?'

'None at all. When I get into the office, there are a few letters I have to write for the Holcomb Line, so there'll be company stuff to send off as well. What about you, Charlotte?'

'I've a letter for Lucy too! I'll go up and fetch it...'

When she returned with the letter, her parents and Will were sitting around the parlour table.

'We haven't seen Lucy since little Bea was a babe in arms, of course,' Edith was saying. 'I'd really like to be with her when she nears the time of the new baby's birth. James works such long shifts and she's often alone.'

'Aye, it's a real shame they're so far away,' replied Will sympathetically. 'It's a heck of a journey up into the Lakes.'

'Now my chess table's fixed, you must come over for a game, Will,' remarked Jacob, polishing his spectacles. 'And with Captain Holcomb on the mend, I can look forward to beating him on a regular basis again.'

'When Master saw me working on the table, he said *he* was looking forward to beating *you!*'

'Did he now?' Reverend Vale shook his head. 'It's a sorry state of affairs when a reasonable man like Samuel Holcomb cannot accept he's hopelessly outclassed by a superior chess intellect.'

'I'll pass that on, shall I?'

'Aye. Aye, do that. Give the old devil something to chew over,' said Jacob, chuckling.

'Andrew's back then,' commented Bessie, bustling into the parlour and clattering bowls and spoons on to the table before them.

She fixed her gaze upon Will.

'How does that sit with you? Since Captain Holcomb was took bad, you've gone up in the world a fair step. Does Andrew coming back put your nose out of joint?'

'Bessie!' exclaimed Charlotte, aghast. 'You can't say such things! Besides, it's none of our business!'

'I'm not prying,' retorted the housekeeper stiffly. 'Just concerned about what's to happen to Will now his nibs has seen fit to come home.'

Reverend Vale drew breath to intercede, but Will silenced him with a wry smile.

'It's a fair question. And you're right, Bessie. Miss Hester – and Master, too – have given me a lot of trust and responsibility of late. I don't believe I've let 'em down, but I'll likely go back to doing my old jobs at Gaw Hill now Andrew's here.'

'That's why he's come home then, is it?' persisted Bessie, hand on hip. 'To take over the Holcomb Line?'

'He hadn't received news of his father's illness,' Charlotte put in, stirring honey into her porridge. 'It came as a complete shock to him.'

There was a sudden silence in the cheery parlour, broken only by the shifting of coals in the fire and Bessie Proud's sharp intake of breath.

'Jacob and I didn't see Andrew last night,' ventured Edith awkwardly, addressing Will. 'Charlotte said he looked well.'

'He did, but I've not seen him since. He wasn't up when I came out this morning. But as I understand it, him and Master were in the library until all hours last night, jawing and having a high old time of it!'

'It's his inheritance that's brought him home then, is it?' remarked Bessie thoughtfully, pursing her lips. 'He must have come back to get his money. I bet he didn't bargain on finding his father practically on his death bed, the Holcomb Line all to pot – no disrespect to you or Hester, Will – and everyone taking it for granted he'll step right into the Captain's shoes!'

'To speak of Andrew this way is monstrous! It's unfair and unkind of you, Bessie!' declared Charlotte, her voice rising emotionally. 'I'm sure he'll do everything in his power to help his family now they need him!'

'Huh!' Bessie snorted derisively. 'He was always wayward, as we know. Mark my words, time will tell whether Andrew Holcomb faces up to his responsibilities – or collects his money, cuts and runs!'

A Sinister Stranger

Charlotte stood waiting her turn in Entwistle's, staring blankly at the shelves and drawers, bottles, jars and boxes lining the walls of the well-stocked grocer's shop in Hild Head.

She'd expected Andrew to come to see her that first day after he'd arrived home. However he had not appeared. Nor had he come the next day or the one after that.

Neither had she seen Will since he'd brought back Pa's chess table, so she had no way of knowing what was going on at Gaw Hill.

Why on earth hadn't Andrew been in touch—

'I said, are you coming in for Zeb Lumby's ale later?' repeated Judith Poulsom, nudging Charlotte's arm as she squeezed past her with a laden basket. 'Eee, you were miles away then, lass!'

'Sorry, Judith!' She smiled apologetically at the landlord's wife. 'As soon as I've finished my errands I'll come into The Bear before I start my rounds.'

Charlotte duly made her purchases. Some of the groceries were for the parsonage, but mostly they were for parishioners like Zeb Lumby and Widow Tunstall, who were poorly or aged, and found it difficult to get out and about, especially in winter.

When the errands were done, the ale collected from The Bear and delivered to Mr Lumby, and Charlotte's round of visits to her father's parishioners were completed, she and Snuffy took the short cut through the beech wood to St Hild's.

On her hands and knees in the deserted church, she began polishing the heavily carved mahogany pulpit. Gradually, the steady, methodical rhythm and stillness of her task soothed Charlotte's agitated spirits and she was scarcely aware of the west door creaking open.

'Thank goodness! You *are* here! I called at the parsonage and your mother said you'd either be out in the parish or in church–' Andrew strode up the nave towards her. 'I've trailed around the whole of Hild Head seeking you out– Good Lord, Lottie– Must you do that?'

'Someone has to,' she replied evenly,

biting back the impulse to run straight to him. 'And it's satisfying, helping the church look its best.'

'If you say so.' He surveyed her, unconvinced. 'But aren't there local women who can do that sort of thing?'

'Yes, there are,' she replied, 'and I'm one of them. Several of us take turns – including Ma and your sister! Besides, I like to spend time alone here – it's a good place to think.'

'I'm far from sure that's a good thing,' he remarked grimly, sweeping off his hat and cloak and tossing them across the nearest pew. 'I've done little else of late, and definitely wouldn't recommend thinking as an entertaining diversion.'

Extending his hands, he drew Charlotte up from her knees and bent to kiss her cheek.

'I'm so sorry I haven't been to visit you... There's been so much... Can you forgive me?'

She gazed up into his solemn eyes, and her heart went out to him.

'Is everything well at Gaw Hill? With the Captain and Hester, I mean?'

'Well enough,' he replied, not releasing her hands. 'Come spend the rest of the day with me, Lottie! We could take a drive. Go into town and eat pastries at the Viennese coffee shop. Do some shopping, whatever you choose…'

'I'm not dressed for going into town!' She brushed down her skirts and retrieved the polishing cloth from the floor.

'How long will it take you to put away your dusting cloths and don your best bonnet?' he persisted, adding earnestly, 'Come on, Lottie. I've had a thoroughly miserable time since I got back to Hild Head – I need your company. Please don't disappoint me!'

It was a dry but bitterly cold day, with insufficient wind blowing in from the German Ocean to stir the sails of the vessels at anchor in the harbour. The Holcombs' smart gig was briskly following the drover's track above Jonas Rock and simply being at Andrew's side had dispelled Charlotte's earlier gloom, despite the melancholy of his own mood.

'…And I have to confess, when you told me Father had been unwell, I wasn't overly concerned,' he was saying as the roofs of the old town came into view. 'Father's had several spells of poor health over the years and I hadn't imagined this bout any more serious than the earlier ones… But when I got up to Gaw Hill and actually *saw* him…'

'It must have been a great shock to you,

Andrew,' she murmured sympathetically. 'But Doctor Hawkes is pleased with his progress.'

'Seeing him in that contraption ... looking so old and frail... It shook me.' His dark eyes met hers sidelong. 'Father's face is paler than wax, Lottie, and somehow bloodless!'

'The doctor insists your father's health will remain stable providing he does not overtax himself,' she went on softly. 'Your being here will surely speed his recuperation!'

Andrew smiled. 'The old man and I have always rubbed along reasonably well. The problem is that he assumes I'll be staying in Hild Head and taking over the company.'

Charlotte gasped. 'You're surely not going away again?'

He didn't answer at once.

'You're aware I came into a considerable inheritance upon my twenty-first birthday? When I came back from America, it was to gain control of my money. I had no thought of even joining the Holcomb Line, much less of taking charge of it!'

'Andrew!' she cried, aghast. 'It's what your family expects of you!'

'Oh, I'm *well* aware of that!' he remarked caustically. 'While I was in Carolina, somebody observed I may have been born and bred to commerce, but by nature was truly a gentleman of leisure given to the pursuit of pleasure. Now I admit, the Southerners do have a flowery way with words, but the point was well made.

'I've never wanted to run the Holcomb Line but suddenly it's thrust upon me. And Father is too ill for me to tell him I don't want it. I feel utterly trapped, Lottie. Whatever am I to do?'

'You have no choice, Andrew. It's your duty and your family needs you.'

'I might've guessed you'd be dreadfully sensible!'

'Have you been into the Holcomb Line office yet? Then why not visit there today – even if for no better reason than it will please the Captain to know you've been?' she encouraged. 'You have to start somewhere, and there really isn't any sense in putting it off.'

And so he slowed the gig as they entered the town, veering towards the waterfront where the Holcomb Line had its chambers.

Drawing close to the Crown Buildings, Andrew looked up at the imposing, grimy façade.

'I'd never have believed this would be my destiny,' he murmured, helping her down.

'Wish me luck–' He broke off, and Charlotte felt his arm reaching protectively about her shoulders as a thickly-set man, who'd been approaching along the pavement in their direction, suddenly stopped dead in his tracks, blocking their progress.

She heard Andrew draw a sharp breath, but the swarthy man spoke first.

'Well, well! If it isn't Mister Andrew Holcomb!' He spoke with a heavy Portuguese accent. 'I never thought to see your face again in Whitby!'

'Out of my way, sir!' ordered Andrew through his teeth.

'Just as you say. But I'll be seeing you again, I have no doubt. Good day to you, miss.' With excessive gallantry, the man doffed his hat in Charlotte's direction.

Charlotte realised she was gripping Andrew's arm fiercely. Despite the man's overt politeness, there'd been something thoroughly unpleasant about the encounter. *Menacing*, almost. She glanced over her shoulder to see the stranger crossing the street and disappearing into a narrow alley lined with grog shops, eating-houses and poor lodgings.

'Andrew– Who was that awful man?'

'I have no idea,' he replied dismissively.

'I've never seen him before.'

'But he knew you– He knew your name!'

'He may indeed know me, but I certainly do not know him!'

'He seemed to remember you from before you left for America,' she persisted, glancing once more over her shoulder. 'Whatever did he mean when he said he'd surely see you again?'

'I've absolutely no notion what a cut-throat like him might mean,' returned Andrew tersely. 'Now come along, Lottie. Let us do what we came to do.'

'Master Andrew!' the head clerk, Jenkins, was immediately on his feet as they walked into the Holcomb Line offices. 'We'd heard you were back. Welcome home.'

'Many thanks, Jenkins,' Andrew responded, his gaze sweeping the cramped office. 'Miss Vale and I–'

'Tim! Will you take this to Mr Munabar at the Saracen's Head–' The door of the inner office had swung open and Will strode out, a sealed packet in his hand.

He halted before reaching the boy's high desk in the corner.

'Charlotte! Andrew! What are you–?' He stepped aside, gesturing that they should enter Captain Holcomb's office.

'Mr Jenkins, can you fetch us some tea?'

'Not for us, Will. We're on our way to the Viennese coffee house.'

Will passed the sealed package to the office boy, speaking quietly.

'Quick as you can, Tim! Be sure to give it to Mr Munabar yourself and wait for his reply.'

Andrew smiled as he followed Charlotte through to his father's dimly-lit, old-fashioned office, where a fierce-looking portrait of Samuel Holcomb, with images of his ships in the background, hung above a massive fireplace.

Will soon came after them, closing the door behind him.

'There's nowt wrong at Gaw Hill? With the Captain?' he asked anxiously.

'Everything's fine, old boy,' reassured Andrew, gazing round the room and getting his bearings. 'Father tells me the company would likely have gone under but for your efforts and loyalty since his illness.'

Will refused to accept the compliment.

'Miss Hester would never allow that to happen. I was able to lend a hand with routine stuff, nothing more. So, when are you taking over, Andrew?'

Andrew expelled a slow breath and shrugged.

'I'm not in any hurry, truth to tell.'

'But you are coming in to run the company?' persisted Will, an edge coming to his quiet voice. 'Master will never be the man he was. For all his bluster and fine talk, he knows he'll never again have strength enough to run this business. That's *your* job, Andrew!'

'Will!' admonished Charlotte gently. 'Andrew has just arrived home! Simply because he chooses not to rush into things doesn't mean he takes his responsibilities lightly and you should not imply he does!'

'Will is quite right, Lottie. But to answer his question, I'm not yet sure when I'll be taking over. This is all quite unexpected.'

'Unexpected?' echoed Will, looking annoyed. 'You've always known the company would come–' he broke off as a timid tap upon the door presaged the return of Tim, offering an envelope.

Will tore it open at once, and looked pleased as he read the letter within.

'Good news?' asked Charlotte, impressed by this authoritative manner that she'd never seen Will display before.

'New business for the Holcomb Line,' he

returned with a smile. 'For months, the company has been chasing a contract for transporting spices. Finally, we've got the merchant's signature!' He passed the pages across to Andrew. 'Take it home with you, Andrew. Master and Hester will be pleased to see that one signed. And, besides, you'll be dealing with Munabar a fair bit in the future. He's a slippery customer, but he's got his head screwed on right and can put a lot of business our – the company's – way!'

'I'll take your word for it,' replied Andrew, pocketing the letter. 'We'll leave you to your business. Come, Charlotte– The Viennese coffee house awaits!'

They quit the office and walked back to the gig, each lost in their own thoughts.

'Not still fretting about our sinister Portuguese friend, are you?' asked Andrew unexpectedly.

'Hmm? Oh, no. I was thinking about Will,' she answered simply. 'How differently he behaved today – from the way I think of him, that is. It made me remember something Hester once said; that Will has the ability to rise in the world and be anything he chooses. I didn't really pay too much attention then, but she was absolutely right, wasn't she?'

'My sister has the irritating habit of always

being right,' commented Andrew. 'To be fair, though, Will always was the brighter of the two of us. I had the fine education, but Will worked hard and tried his best at everything he did. I do believe that trait more than any other endears him to my father, and to Hester too.'

'You've often said Will is as close to you as any brother,' ventured Charlotte, briefly resting her head against his shoulder as they settled into the gig and he took up the reins. 'Perhaps you and he could work together at the Holcomb Line? He could help you run the company.'

'Definitely not,' returned Andrew with unexpected conviction. 'If I'm to run the company, I'll do it without interference from Will, Hester or even my father. The Holcomb line would be mine alone and I alone would control it!'

They took refreshment at Mr Werner's Viennese coffee house and then strolled arm-in-arm through the chill afternoon air, browsing the elegant shops in the curving sweep of Bishopsgate.

'Shall we call into Ransome's?' enquired Andrew, pausing outside a very grand double-fronted shop. 'You do still like chocolate, don't you?'

'Of course!'

'Come along, then!' He laughed down at her as they entered the premises of the chocolatier. 'What is it to be? Turkish delight? Fruit cups? Brazil snaps? Russian toffee?'

Charlotte had loved Ransome's ever since childhood. The shop's bay windows were filled with dozens of different kinds of sweet-meats displayed upon dishes with lace doilies. It was also a shop you never actually entered, for its goods were so fearfully expensive!

As they went inside, a middle-aged woman dressed in mourning clothes and with a small girl at her side was leaving.

'Miss Vale! Good afternoon!' she said pleasantly. 'How are you?'

'Very well, thank you,' responded Charlotte, making the necessary introductions before continuing. 'We haven't seen you for a while, Mrs Burdon. Sophy has been greatly missed in the choir at St Hild's!'

'My three girls all enjoy music, but Sophy really does love to sing! I believe it's her greatest joy,' returned Clara Burdon with a smile, adding reflectively. 'We had occasion to return briefly to Egleton, Miss Vale. Family business of sorts. I'm afraid the visit stirred many memories of happier times. Although our steward is a good enough man and certainly does his best, it was extremely distressing to see the old place looking so forlorn. Egleton needs people and activity to bring it back to life.' Mrs Burdon paused. 'How is all at St Hild's? Has Miss Holcomb been successful in prevailing upon Mr Rowbourne to sing at our Advent concert?'

'Yes, indeed!' Charlotte beamed. 'Hester received a charming reply to her letter. Mr Rowbourne said he'll be pleased to sing at St Hild's and will even bring some of his own musicians!'

'How marvellous!'

'Will we see you in church this Sunday?' ventured Charlotte after a moment. 'And Sophy, too?'

'All being well!' responded the older woman. 'The younger girls and I will certainly be at St Hild's for services, but poor Sophy is recovering from a troublesome head cold so might not be able to attend. That's really the reason we came into town today, to choose her favourite chocolates in an effort to cheer her spirits!'

'Please do give her my regards,' replied Charlotte. 'I hope she'll be feeling better very soon...'

Andrew bent to murmur into Charlotte's ear as Mrs Burdon and her youngest daughter left the chocolate maker's shop. 'I don't recall meeting her before– And I'm sure I *would've* remembered, gentry isn't exactly thick on the ground in Hild Head!'

'Mrs Burdon is widowed. She and her three daughters only removed here from Wharfedale last year,' replied Charlotte quietly. 'They live right on the edge of Hild Head in The Crescent overlooking the town.'

'The Crescent? They're very elegant new houses, as I recall. Mind, for all she's in mourning still, Mrs Burdon herself was extremely elegant and fashionably turned-out,' he commented, adding as he fended off a blow from Charlotte's glove. 'Not that I really noticed, of course. Have you chosen your chocolates yet?'

'All done,' she replied, adding blithely, 'Don't you think Hester might like some chocolates, too?'

'I *hadn't* thought about it, actually.'

'Then perhaps you should!' She continued more earnestly, 'These past months have been very difficult for her. She works hard and never gives a thought to herself. Her whole life is bound up with her family and

79

home and the parish and doing things for others.'

'Can sainthood be far away for my dear sister?' he mused sarcastically.

'I'm serious, Andrew! I know you and she have never got along well; however, if it were not for Hester – and Will, too – there'd hardly be a Holcomb Line for you to come back to!'

He arched an eyebrow. 'In the past, you never cared much for Hester. May I ask what has brought about this considerable change of heart?'

'I used to dislike her because you did. When I was younger, I was a little afraid of her too. She seemed so strict and fierce.' Charlotte lowered her eyes. 'Then, after your father was taken ill, she and I spent a lot of time together. I got to know and like Hester very much.' She concluded simply, 'The small treat of some chocolates would be a kind gesture.'

'Very well. She shall have her chocolates. But only because you wish it.'

'And take care to offer them to her graciously!'

'Lottie! I've caved in to giving her chocolates, I'm not making rash promises about graciousness as well. Now choose whatever you think suitable for the old girl. My suggestion would be acid drops.'

'Andrew! You're incorrigible.'

'I am,' he agreed, lowering his face and stealing the lightest kiss.

Andrew Goes Missing

Christmas was fast approaching, and as Charlotte and her mother decked the parlour with pine cones and evergreen boughs, their conversation was very much about the forthcoming festivities.

'I must get Lucy and James's pudding and bunloaf packed up and ready to send this week,' Edith Vale was saying, weaving glossy variegated ivy along the mantel and behind the clock and trinkets.

'I finished knitting Bea's mittens and bonnet weeks ago. And Lucy's bed-jacket only needs pressing, so they're ready to go,' replied Charlotte, stepping back to consider the sprays of holly and laurel she was arranging. 'I really must go into town soon, too. We need more cloves, and some cinnamon sticks and other bits and bobs from the spice merchant.'

Taking up a basket filled with ribbons, coloured strips of paper and tiny silver bells, Edith sat at the fireside, moving aside the knitting Charlotte had left on the cushioned seat of the rocking chair.

'My word, Will's jumper is certainly coming along! Is this your last sleeve?'

'Mmm, I'm not sure about the colour, though,' replied Charlotte, glancing over her shoulder to where her mother was beginning to twist the ribbons and pleated paper into garlands. 'I chose it because Will always brings me a bunch of heather whenever he's out on the moors.'

'It's a good, manly colour and the dye has taken well,' replied Edith, considering the sleeve. 'He'll be delighted with it – not least, because *you've* made it for him!'

'Actually, I've been hurrying to finish it,' said Charlotte. 'A few days ago, I bumped into him on the beach and noticed how threadbare his woollen has become. I'm giving him his jumper as soon as it's ready, instead of waiting until Christmas Day.'

'That's a sensible idea,' remarked her mother thoughtfully, adding, 'He hasn't looked his usual cheery self of late, has he?'

'I really haven't seen much of him, Ma, apart from that once on the beach,' answered Charlotte, returning to the fireside and taking a share of ribbons and pleated paper from the basket. 'And I've hardly seen Andrew at all recently! He seems to spend every minute in Whitby!'

'That's only to be expected. Taking over the running of his family business is no small task for a young man, and I daresay the huge responsibility is weighing heavily upon him.'

'Oh, I'm sure it is! Hester was telling me he hasn't eaten his evening meal at home in weeks. He stays late in town every night and hardly ever returns before the rest of the household is abed! Meanwhile, I'm wondering whatever I might give him for Christmas!' went on Charlotte, twisting ribbon and paper. 'This is his first Christmas at home for years and I'd love to give him something really special. I expect while he was staying in Carolina with the Duchesneys, he became accustomed to sophisticated, expensive gifts.'

'Remember, the simplest present often brings the most heartfelt sentiment!' commented Edith.

'Ma, do you think I might make Andrew a shirt? A really nice, fancy one?'

'Is there enough time?' considered Edith, also recalling that while Andrew had always been well-dressed, he'd returned to Hild Head very much the fashionable gentleman about town and, according to Bessie Proud,

84

frequented the finest tailor in the whole of Yorkshire.

'Yes, Ma. I have got enough time because,' she lowered her voice, despite their being alone in the parlour, 'I've nearly finished Pa's Christmas nightshirt – there're only the buttonholes and buttons to do. When I go into town for the spices, I will look around for some fine material for Andrew's shirt.'

'Your pa was telling me that Hester's tenor is coming to the next choir practice at St Hild's,' remarked Edith after a moment, tying off the loose ends of the bright, shining garland. 'I'd imagined he'd just turn up on the night of the Advent concert and sing!'

'That's what everyone thought, so it's causing quite a stir with the choir!' responded Charlotte. 'However, when Mr Rowbourne asked Hester if he might bring a small group of his own musicians with him and attend the next choir practice to rehearse his pieces for the concert, she could hardly refuse.

'It's going to be a much grander affair than any of us expected, and everyone's starting to get very nervous. There's to be a reception up at Gaw Hill, too. That was Andrew's idea. Hester had planned to invite Mr Rowbourne and his musicians for a quiet supper after the concert. However, Andrew said that wasn't how things were done and now there is to be a proper dinner and party and everything with lots of guests!'

'As if Hester hasn't enough to do!' muttered Edith. 'And she's never been one for entertaining. We must see if we can lend a hand, Charlotte.'

'I've already offered, Ma. She is in a bit of a flurry–' Charlotte broke off at the ring of the bell and rose from the fireside. 'That'll be Will bringing Captain Holcomb to visit Pa. I'll get the door and make their tea. Bessie's still out in the wash house...'

Later that week, leaving Snuffy behind at the parsonage, Charlotte wrapped up warmly against the cutting offshore wind and set off upon the long walk into Whitby.

As she strode briskly along the cliff path she turned over in her mind her list of festive errands. The heavy box of Christmas presents for Lucy and her family needed to be sent off upon the northbound coach. Three – no, four items had to be purchased from the spice merchant. She needed to get baccy for Pa, and some for Captain Holcomb, too, although he favoured a stronger pipe than Reverend Vale. She also required almonds, so that she might grind them and make a marchpane cake, which was always her gift to her mother at Christmastide and birthdays. Flower water was required from the perfumer for Hester, and she would also visit each of the town's mercers in search of the right material for Andrew's shirt.

'Wait!'

She turned around. 'Pa!'

'I've been waiting for the chance to catch you somewhere on your own–' puffed the Reverend, trotting along the winding path through the churchyard and catching up with Charlotte as she passed the east gate on the cliff path. 'Somewhere your ma can't hear us.'

Charlotte rested Lucy's Christmas box on the weather-worn stone wall.

'What is wrong, Pa?'

'It's like this, Charlotte, I've got your ma a nice tea tray for Christmas. I know she's been wanting a new one for a long while now,' he began. 'However, there's another present she'd like more than any other, isn't there?'

He peered at her over the rims of his silver spectacles, and Charlotte nodded.

'Ma would love to visit Lucy, of course. And be with her when the new baby is born.'

'Precisely!' beamed Jacob, clasping his daughter's narrow shoulder. 'I know the child's not due for months yet – and just as well, for the road into the Lakes is often snowed-up during winter – but I want you to go to Lucy's and stay until after the baby comes. You and your ma both!'

'It's a lovely idea, Pa, but the coach fare would cost a fortune!' exclaimed Charlotte. 'Ma must go, but I'll stay here with you!'

'No, Charlotte. I've made up my mind. It's high time you both saw Lucy again and–'

'Ma would never agree to going so far away for weeks and weeks if it meant leaving you alone,' she interrupted gently. 'Besides, Lucy and James's little quarry cottage is two up and two down. There'll barely be room for Ma. It wouldn't be fair on them for me to turn up, too.'

'That makes sense enough, I suppose,' he conceded, a mite disappointed.

'But you couldn't give Ma a better present!' smiled Charlotte, giving her father a quick hug. 'Lucy will be thrilled, too. Are you sure we can afford it, though? The coach fare for a seat inside is awfully expensive!'

'I'm certainly not about to let your ma sit up top with her baggage!' chuckled Jacob. 'I did that myself several times when I was a young curate, and it's a bit too much of an adventure! No, I'm sure we'll have enough money,' he went on seriously. 'I've had this notion in mind for some time so I've been putting a bit by each week. Your mother's a remarkable woman, Charlotte. She puts up with always having to scrimp and make do without a word of complaint. Just this once, I want to give her a real treat.

'I intend writing a little note about the trip, and I'll put it with her other Christmas presents – so we must keep it a surprise until then,' he finished, pushing his hands deep into the pockets of his coat, his face flushed with excitement and the bitter wind. 'Then at the end of the winter, before the baby is due, your ma can be off and on her way!'

They parted, with Reverend Vale taking the short-cut across country into Hild Head while Charlotte continued on her way along the cliff path and down into Whitby.

Thoughts of her mother's forthcoming trip kept her company as she strode along the high ground past the abbey ruins. The family lived comfortably at the parsonage, but actual money was always in short supply and she knew, despite Pa's reassurances, that their finances would be stretched, just by providing the coach fare alone.

Charlotte chewed her lip. Ma already needed new boots, and for such a long, cold journey, a warm coat and muff would be practically a necessity.

By mid-morning, she was making her way down into the town. It was market day and even busier there than usual. She spent the next few hours shopping and browsing shop windows and stalls, choosing a wooden rattle with smooth beads for Lucy's new baby, before scouring the mercers and finally selecting the best shirting she could afford.

Pausing at the shoemakers, she glanced at the fine dancing slippers, elegant pumps and robust boots.

The latter would be ideal for Ma, and perfect for her trip to the Lakes. And while choosing the material for Andrew's shirt, Charlotte had noticed bolts of stout woollen stuff that would make a sturdy winter coat for her mother. She and Bessie could sew it together. Ma sorely needed a new coat...

Her last stop was to purchase the fine almonds for the marchpane cake and, after coming out from the shop and ensuring her purchases and purse were safe from the thieves and pickpockets who prowled the bustling streets, she continued along Bishopsgate.

Passing by the Viennese coffee house with its tantalising aromas of freshly-ground coffee beans and continental pastries, she paused to take in the windows of the gold merchants, with their gleaming displays of jewellery, unset gemstones, old gold and jet ornaments.

She was admiring a chess set carved from jet and ivory when she noticed a discreet notice in the corner of the next-door milliner's shop window. A vacancy existed. Full training would be given. Applications were invited within...

Charlotte stood stock still on the teeming street, staring at the neatly printed notice. A sudden rush of excitement bubbled up inside her. If she had paid employment she'd be able to afford winter boots and perhaps a length of quality stuff for a warm coat, too...

She hovered uncertainly, having no idea what might be expected of her when she entered the bright little shop; however, swallowing her nerves, she pushed open the low door of Prentise Millinery and went inside.

Twenty minutes later, she emerged elated.

She was to begin working there at the start of next week! Walking as though on air, with little thought of direction, she realised she was but a few minutes away from the Crown Buildings and impulsively turned toward the waterfront. Excited and pleased with her news, she hastened into the formidable building. Only when she reached the frosted glass door did she hesitate about disturbing Andrew at his work.

As she stood deliberating, the door was pulled open and the office boy almost barged into her, his arms filled with bundles of post. From within the office, Jenkins looked up and saw her. Before she could do anything more, she was politely shown straight into Captain Holcomb's old office.

'Will!' she exclaimed, as Jenkins deferentially closed the door behind her. 'I didn't expect to find you here! I didn't realise you still came into the office!'

'I don't,' he replied shortly, pushing a hand through his unruly hair as he shoved aside the mass of papers spread across the huge mahogany desk. 'And if it's Andrew you're looking for, then I'm afraid you're out of luck. Nobody's seen him since this time yesterday.'

'Where is he?' she queried, her own news

temporarily forgotten.

'Pshaw! Your guess is as good as mine!' He pushed back his chair, flexing stiffness from his shoulders. 'He didn't return home last night. But Andrew can take care of himself, it's Caesar I'm concerned about. He treats that horse like a machine.' He broke off, and grimaced at her apologetically. 'Sorry, lass. I didn't mean to bite your head off. Sit yourself down, and your bundles too. By, but you've been busy today! Can I get you some tea?'

'No, thank you,' she answered absently, her brow creased. 'You say Andrew didn't return to Gaw Hill last night? Have you been out looking for him? Suppose he's had an accident? Or–'

'Don't fret yourself,' interrupted Will easily. 'If Caesar had come home on his own, then I'd have got up a party to search for his owner. Nowt's happened to Andrew. He knows his way around this town better than most.'

'But something must have happened if he hasn't been into the office!' she argued loyally. 'You know how diligent he's been since he took over! Hester's told me how he always works late!'

'Stays in town late, aye,' remarked Will

93

darkly. 'Works late? Well, happen that's another story!'

'Will, don't be so unfair! You know how hard Andrew's been working!'

'Then maybe the novelty's wearing off,' he said coldly. 'I asked Jenkins, and apparently young Mr Holcomb has taken to leaving the office at around noon, not to be seen for the rest of the day!'

'You questioned his staff about him? I'm ashamed of you, Will!'

'I'm sorry you feel that way,' he returned stiffly. 'But if Andrew was pulling his weight, then he'd be here like he should be. As it turned out, it's lucky I was here – somebody had to be! You need to open your eyes and see him for what he really is, Charlotte – not as you'd like him to be.'

'That's a horrible thing to say!'

'You're in love with him, Charlotte!' he retorted bitterly. 'You've always loved him. Saw only good in him! Even that night when he sailed for America–'

Will broke off, and turned away. Rising from the mahogany desk, he paced the room.

'I don't want us to argue, Charlotte. I just don't want you to be hurt.'

'I'm sure if something has gone wrong,'

she said quietly, 'then it's been an honest mistake. Andrew would not let anybody down.'

She heard Will's ragged intake of breath, and for a long moment the only sounds in the old office were the shift of coals on the fire, the hum of voices from without and the howl of seagulls wheeling out across the German Ocean.

'Let me tell you something, Charlotte. Long before he was taken ill, Captain Holcomb had been trying to get Gerard Lassiter to use the Holcomb Line for shipping his sailcloth,' stated Will. 'Lassiter makes a superior kind of sailcloth,' he explained. 'It's expensive and much sought after in the ports far beyond Whitby. He's got a mill on Norway Street that employs forty-odd workers and has all the new machinery and looms. Master's been chasing his sailcloth business for years, but Lassiter's a canny devil and was content with the arrangement he had with the Baltic Star company.

'Then, a few months back, shortly after the Captain was taken to his bed, Hester got word that all was not well with Lassiter and the Baltic Star. There'd been some sort of falling out. Anyhow, Hester's not one to let the grass grow under her feet and, between

95

us, her and me got on to Lassiter and made him an offer to carry his sailcloth.'

'And?'

'After months of shilly-shallying, he finally agreed to the contract. He sent word he'd be here first thing this morning to sign the papers. The deal was done, Charlotte,' went on Will tersely. 'All Andrew had to do was be here, sign the papers, shake Lassiter's hand and take his money!'

'I'm sure he *would've* been here … perhaps he didn't know about the meeting.'

'For pity's sake, stop making excuses for him!' retorted Will angrily. 'Andrew simply couldn't be bothered turning up!'

'But surely–'

'When there was no sign of him at Gaw Hill this morning, I told Miss Hester I'd best get into town and be ready to meet Lassiter just in case Andrew didn't appear. Muggins here had to carry the can and make the apologies. Lassiter is a superior beggar and he was expecting to see the owner of the Line, not his hired hand! We came *this* close to losing that sailcloth contract!'

'I'm sorry it's been so difficult for you,' she responded stiffly. 'However, your only concern is this wretched contract! Don't you realise Andrew might have had an accident or been taken ill? You don't seem to care at all that anything might have happened to him!'

'I'm pretty certain of the shape and form of what's happened to him,' retorted Will grimly. 'And I've spent today trying to put right other stuff he's let slide. Anyhow, that's not your worry, nor mine either if it comes down to it. Now, I know you came to see Andrew, but is there anything I can do?'

She shook her head, her news no longer seemed worth telling. In addition, she'd been shocked by Will's uncharacteristic harshness.

'I'll be here a good few hours more,' he was saying now, 'but if you leave your parcels, I'll bring them by the parsonage on my way up to Gaw Hill this evening.'

'There's no need. They aren't heavy,' she replied as she rose to leave. 'Will, I can't agree with what you've said about Andrew, but I don't want us to fall out. Please call at the parsonage on your way home and stay for supper – if you're not expected at Gaw Hill, that is.'

'I've nobody waiting on me, Charlotte,' he replied quietly, showing her to the door. 'Thanks for the invitation, but I'll likely be late.'

'That doesn't matter. Bessie can keep the

food hot, and we can eat together in the kitchen if Pa and Ma have already had their meal. Please come, Will.'

'Aye, I will.' He reached for the door, adding in the seconds before he opened it. 'And don't worry for Andrew. I fancy he was expecting to stay out. He'll have come to no harm.'

Charlotte searched his face and would've questioned him further but the door was open and the opportunity lost. 'I pray you're right. Until tonight.'

Along the dusky waterfront, Charlotte was waiting amongst the market day crush to cross over the street when she spied somebody she recalled all too keenly. It was the man who had accosted Andrew and herself outside the Crown Buildings and he was coming out of a tavern on the opposite side of the road.

Charlotte gasped, for stooping to clear the tavern's low doorway and following the foreigner out on to the corner was Andrew! His clothing was creased and dishevelled, his thick hair untidy, and he was clearly unshaven, but otherwise he appeared quite himself and unharmed.

She could scarcely believe her eyes,

because the two men were obviously on good terms. They paused outside the Black Jack Tavern to conclude their conversation, shaking hands amiably before parting, and then the foreigner went back inside while Andrew put on his hat and, striding around the corner, disappeared down the arched ghaut towards the stables.

He emerged again almost at once, riding Caesar at a walk along the congested street. Charlotte watched him pass by as she stood in the crowd, following him with her eyes. Once clear of the traffic and milling crowds, Andrew kicked his horse into a trot, and headed up into the shadows of the cliff path toward Hild Head.

Bessie Proud was in on the secret about Ma's trip to the Lakes and, with Christmas little more than a week away, there was much whispering while she and Charlotte were busy in the kitchen.

'I still keep pinching myself,' exclaimed Charlotte, pressing Will's jumper with the flat iron as they talked. 'Mrs Prentise said I was hard-working and helpful, and that my first week had gone so well she'll be keeping me on until her niece comes back!

'I really enjoy the work and, because Mrs

Prentise doesn't need me at the shop every day, I've still enough time for my parish rounds. I daren't fall behind with those. Especially at this time of year when so many people are coming down poorly.'

Snuffy ran to the door, whining and wagging her tail, and Charlotte hastily wrapped the jumper into a parcel while Bessie went to let in Will.

He strode down the passage through to the kitchen, bundled against the cold in his homespuns, and bringing with him into the warm kitchen something of the keen winter's day.

'Kettle's on to boil,' Bessie told him, bustling away into the scullery. 'Miss Charlotte'll see to you – I've things to do!'

While Will warmed himself at the fireside, Charlotte set tea, a plate of bannocks still warm from the oven, a dish of butter and pot of honey on to the scrubbed kitchen table.

'I know there's still a while to go before the day, but the weather's so cold.' She offered the parcel, stooping to give him a quick kiss on the cheek. 'Happy Christmas, Will!'

Unwrapping the parcel, his face broke into a wide smile. 'It's grand, Charlotte! Really grand! I like these fancy patterns in the wool. I've not had anything like this before!'

'They're called cables, and that one is a feather twist,' she explained, pointing it out. 'You use a special sort of needle for it.'

'Can I put it on?'

'Of course!'

Once, not so very long ago, they'd hugged as friends without a second thought; but now Will hesitated before embracing her awkwardly.

'I'll not feel cold down on the beach at all! Thanks, Charlotte.'

'Drink your tea.' She smiled, pleased. 'While I put on my boots and coat...'

The beach was bleak and deserted, the tide just a distant grey sliver as they scoured the shore below Hild Head cliffs gathering sea-coal washed up by the previous night's high water.

'How's your job in the hat shop?' enquired Will, glancing at Charlotte's rosy face as she bent to collect the small pieces of coal which she then threw into one of the sacks that Will was pulling along on a sled.

'Fine! I was just telling Bessie about it. I've had my very first wages! I've put a deposit on a pair of winter boots for Ma. I'll pay a little each week and the shoemaker will hold them for me. After that, I'm going to buy some merino for Ma's new coat.'

'I've never seen you looking happier,' commented Will, considering her sidelong before hefting another sack of sea-coal on to the sled. 'But I daresay that's all down to Andrew being home, isn't it?'

Charlotte blushed. 'It has been wonderful since he came back. We haven't spent much time together recently, but, well, do – do you suppose he knows how I feel about him, Will?'

'Oh, aye, I'm certain of it! Andrew knows all right,' he remarked, adding, 'Charlotte, don't take this amiss, but don't … don't...'

'Don't what?'

'Ah, I don't know!' He exhaled heavily. 'Andrew has always marched to his own tune. Half the time I've no idea where he is or what he's up to.'

Will said nothing more, but his comments had resurrected Charlotte's misgivings at seeing Andrew emerging from the Black Jack Tavern with the foreigner. She'd never asked him about it. There never seemed to be the right moment, for she wouldn't want him to feel she was prying into his affairs.

Besides, any such misgivings that she had, vanished like mist in sunlight whenever

Andrew came to her and smiled down into her eyes, touching his lips to her cheek and taking her arm in his.

She couldn't deny the surge of pride she felt at being seen with him in the Viennese coffee house, or at the long assembly room in The Old White Bear, or simply strolling from church, when she was aware of envious glances from Sophy Burdon and other girls who openly admired the handsome man at Charlotte's side.

Now, Charlotte watched thoughtfully as Snuffy mooched along the foot of the cliff while Will slung a twisted rope harness about his shoulders and began hauling the sled across the wet sand. They passed by the steps cut into the cliff face, walking on another half-mile or so to a narrow path snaking away up to the cliff's top.

'How are you getting on, Will?' she asked, meeting his eyes solemnly. *'Really*, I mean.'

'Once Andrew came home, things were bound to change. He's the only son and as such is heir to the company,' replied Will at length. 'If he'd taken over and I'd gone back to my old jobs at Gaw Hill, I could've accepted that – but Andrew doesn't pull his weight, Charlotte!'

'It's more than Andrew neglecting his

duties at the company though,' she ventured. 'Something's badly wrong, isn't it?'

He frowned. 'I've never thought myself an ambitious man. I wanted to better myself, right enough. Reading, writing, reckoning and such like. Being able to understand politics and what's said in debates at The Old White Bear. Talking about the books and papers your pa lends me. Aye, all that's important to me but, by and large, I were content with my lot.'

'Then Captain Holcomb took ill,' put in Charlotte gently. 'And you were practically running the company – Hester was extremely impressed, she told me so.'

'I wouldn't have known where to start without Miss Hester explaining everything and telling me what to do, and I admit the responsibility scared me to begin with,' reflected Will frankly. 'Then I started to enjoy it. Realised I was good at it. I liked having such things to think about.'

'Hester says you can do anything you put your mind to, Will.'

'Yes, well, when Andrew took over, I missed it, Charlotte. I still miss being part of the Holcomb Line.' He paused thoughtfully. 'I reckon I've taken to resenting Andrew, too.'

'But you still like your work at Gaw Hill?'

'Of course. The Holcombs are my family and Gaw Hill is my home, but I want to *do* something with my life!'

He offered his hand to help her clamber the last yards up the narrow path on to the cliff top where he'd left the pony and wagon sheltered by the churchyard wall from the biting easterly wind. 'I never thought to leave Hild Head, but perhaps I ought to make a fresh start somewhere new. For the first time ever, I don't know my place,' he concluded, his strong features reddened by the cold wind. 'I don't know where I belong, nor where my future lies.'

A Terrible Argument

The last market day before Christmas was always the busiest in Hild Head and Charlotte had risen even earlier than usual in order to leave the parsonage before daybreak.

She wanted to have finished her shopping in the village and be off on her round of parish visits before the market traders filled the square with their stalls, sacks and barrels of goods, livestock and produce, and drew crowds of folk, not only from Hild Head itself, but from the outlying hamlets and villages farther afield that were too small to have a market of their own.

Emerging from Entwistle's with one of her baskets laden with flour, sugar, tea, oats, dried peas, beans and barley, Charlotte checked her list carefully. The potatoes, carrots, turnips and ale could all wait until last because they were the heaviest to carry, but there was still the apothecary to visit.

Hurrying past The Old White Bear, which was already ablaze with lights and activity in readiness for the influx of market day customers, she picked her way across the muddy street and made for the cramped little shop where Archibald Cruickshank sold every kind of medicinal remedy imaginable, from hair restorer to gout relief and cures for freckles.

Charlotte required a bottle of Teething Elixir for Mrs Schofield's new baby, snuff for Widow Tunstall, and a balm for burning ailments in the toes for Mr Duffy whose lifetime of sailing barefoot on the wet decks of fishing boats had left him with fierce pain in his feet.

While Archibald Cruickshank weighed the snuff, Charlotte thought about the visits she needed to make that day.

'I didn't realise you'd taken to inhaling snuff!' The familiar voice was but a whisper close to Charlotte's ear and she smiled, breathing deeply the manly fragrance of Andrew's sandalwood shaving soap. 'Such dark secrets you keep from me, Lottie!'

'I expect you'll be horrified when I buy some coarse chewing tobacco?' She turned to look up at him, her eyes sparkling and her senses suddenly singing at his tantalising closeness. 'Not to mention a flagon of strong ale from The Old White Bear!'

'On the contrary, I do like a woman who

has hobbies. Keeps her out of mischief.' He grinned, taking the most heavily laden of her baskets. 'Lottie! What have you got in here? Why must it be *you* who feeds the starving, clothes the naked and ministers to the afflicted of the parish?'

'Because I'm the vicar's daughter!' she returned with a flounce as he opened the door and they went out into the street. 'Besides, it isn't only me as you well know. Ma and Hester do just as much, if not more, and so do some of the other ladies, including Mrs Burdon and Sophy.'

'If you say so,' he remarked dryly, relieving her of the second basket as they strolled in the general direction of The Old White Bear. 'Although from the little I've seen of Mrs Clara Burdon and her eldest – while I don't doubt they happily bask in the reputation of being ladies bountiful and contribute generous quantities of stockings, and comforters for infants, to the parish poor basket – I somehow cannot see *them* tending sick-beds or spooning gruel!'

'Don't be unkind – the Burdons do what they can,' she admonished mildly. 'And remember, they are still in mourning. I believe Mr Burdon died just last year.'

'Ah yes, precipitating their flight from the

family seat in Wharfedale to take up resi-
dence in the vacant home of long-standing
friends – Hester keeps current with local
gossip,' he added, by way of explaining his
knowledge of the Burdons' circumstances.
'Anyway, how long will you be on these mis-
sions of mercy, Lottie? When I caught sight
of you going into Cruickshank's, I rather
hoped we could steal away for a few hours.
It grieves me we haven't shared more time
together of late.'

'Oh, Andrew! It'd be lovely to spend a day
with you – I only wish I could!' she responded earnestly. 'But I have my rounds. I
know you tease me about it, but there are
folk in Hild Head – especially those like Mr
Duffy along Trimmel Bank – who depend
upon me and Ma and Hester entirely. I can't
let them down, I'm sorry.'

'I'm suitably chastened. To show my
genuine remorse, I'll actually accompany
you as you trail round the desolate quarters
of Hild Head. I can't say fairer than that,
can I?'

'I never can be sure whether you're teasing
or being serious!' she declared. 'You're right
about desolate quarters though, the dwellings along Trimmel Bank are little more
than hovels. It's small wonder that when ill-

ness comes to the village, it finds a strong foothold amongst the folk there. I appreciate your gesture, really I do, but you'd be horribly bored.

'It's not simply a case of knocking upon somebody's door, handing them their goods and rushing away,' she went on soberly. 'Someone might want a fire setting and lighting, food cooking, some cleaning or other chores doing. It's a *visit*, Andrew! Most folk want to talk, and to hear what's going on in the village. They need to feel they're still part of the parish. I don't think your coming with me is a wise idea.'

'You've convinced me utterly.' He took her arm as they crossed the mud-rutted street to The Old White Bear. 'I'll carry your baskets out to the dregs of Hild Head society and then leave you to your devices.'

'I have only to collect the ale and the vegetables, then I'll be on my way...'

Upon leaving the village and the clamour of market day preparations behind, they made steady progress around the inland side of Hild Head.

Presently, their path began to drop down into the valley where the River Trimmel churned and gushed between barren banks to which squat dwellings clung; some windowless, and others with old sailcloth where window apertures had been cut.

'What about tomorrow, Lottie?' asked Andrew as they approached the river. 'Let us make an arrangement to meet.'

'You know tomorrow is one of my hat shop days!'

He groaned. 'Lottie! Must you spend your days peddling hats? It's just not the done thing for a young lady!'

'You're perfectly well aware of my reasons for doing it,' she replied. 'And there shouldn't be anything wrong – not even for young ladies – in working hard to earn an income! You're old-fashioned in your notions, Andrew – you should converse more with Hester!'

'I'd rather drink hemlock. And beware of paying too much heed to my sister's jaundiced view of the order of the world, lest you become as crabbed and resentful as she!'

'I thought you and Hester were getting along rather better than you used to?'

'It didn't last. Now I ignore her as much as possible and confide in her not at all.'

'I'm sorry to hear that.'

'What of tomorrow, then?'

She shook her head. 'Mrs Prentise was

kind enough to take me on and give me a chance, even though I had no experience. I wouldn't dream of letting her down.'

'What about letting me down?' he demanded, fixing her with a gaze that caused her breath to catch in her throat. 'What about what *I* want?'

'Stop trying to make me feel sorry for you!' she said shakily, keeping her tone deliberately light. 'Besides, how could we have spent tomorrow – or today – together?' she finished defensively. 'You'll be busy at your office.'

Andrew's features darkened. 'Lottie, what I do and where I go is my concern. I suppose Will has been whining to you about the way I'm running the company? Well, it's not for Will to comment, is it? He'd do well to remember that!'

'What on earth's got into you?' She was taken aback by his outburst. 'You've recently been spending so much time at the office in Whitby, I merely assumed you'd be there today and tomorrow as usual. I intended no criticism nor intrusion, and I'm sorry if I caused you ill humour!'

'Of course you didn't, and I do beg your pardon,' he responded contritely. 'Now, we have reached our destination and I can deliver you to your errands of mercy. Meanwhile, I'll repair to The Old White Bear and drown my sorrows – but not before I have your promise that we shall spend this evening together? What say you to us driving into town? We could have dinner at the Hotel Excelsior and then go on to the theatre?'

'That would be lovely!' she exclaimed in delight. 'But aren't you attending the debating society at The Old White Bear tonight? It's all about Napoleon's strategy in Spain. Pa's been looking forward to it for weeks. Will is going, too.'

'Is he now? Well, I rather think I shall abstain. The ruminations of some dry-as-dust speaker about far-flung military campaigns are not my idea of an entertainment! May I call for you this evening?'

'Yes, please!' She beamed, pausing at the ancient bridge and taking his hand.

'Splendid! There is just one thing...'

Drawing her into shadowy seclusion beneath the mossy stone bridge, he slowly brought her into his arms. The rushing of the river seemed to fill her senses and she could feel her heartbeat pounding against his chest as he held her tightly. Lowering his mouth to hers in a kiss that swiftly deepened into fierce intensity, leaving her breathless and dizzy when he finally released her.

Aware of the shallow quickness of her breathing, she watched wide-eyed as he gazed down at her, seeing his full lips curve into a slow smile.

'I've waited the longest while to kiss you properly, Lottie. Since that night before I sailed for America, in fact,' His smile widened now, his eyes gleaming in the dappled light as he touched Charlotte's lips once more, this time with the most chaste of kisses.

'It was worth the wait!'

St Hild's parish church had never seen such an occasion as the night before that Christmas Eve. A train of carriages, carts, wagons and folk on foot processed along the cliff path and crowded into the pews or stood gathered around the pillars and arches to hear the Advent concert.

It was a clear, cold night and, clad in her warmest cloak, Charlotte squeezed in at the back of the candlelit church, only to be taken forward to sit with Captain Holcomb and Hester.

The Reverend and Mrs Vale had also been invited into the family pew, as had Mrs Burdon and her two younger daughters – Sophy performing both in the choir and as the solo soprano.

There was no sign of Will, nor of Andrew.

The music was spell-binding, soaring as crisp and clear as the frosty night.

Although she did not consider herself at all musical, Charlotte's heart was singing when the performance was over, and she made her way from the church to Gaw Hill where the supper she had helped prepare lay set out upon seasonally-decked tables.

Congratulations abounded for the Whitby tenor, Edmund Rowbourne, and for the singers and musicians.

Andrew appeared in the dining-room to thank all participants and offered special compliments to Sophy's solo performance.

The festive feast began with warm wassail cups and, although Captain Holcomb was seated at the head of the table, it was Andrew who rose to make the toasts.

Charlotte's heart brimmed with love and pride to see how very handsome he looked and how very graciously he fulfilled the role of host.

It was long past midnight when the evening finally drew to its close and Andrew began making farewells to the guests on behalf of his family.

Sophy bade Charlotte goodnight as they passed in the hall.

'You sang wonderfully,' Charlotte said. 'And what a beautiful dress!'

To her surprise, the other young woman grimaced, lowering her voice.

'I had our maid put new collar and cuffs and bodice buttons upon one of my old dresses – it's so awful not being able to buy new things! It's not so bad for Sally and Susie, because as they grow up they wear my old clothes which at least are of finest quality. But, being eldest, I have to make do with whatever I already have – do tell me I didn't look too plain and homely standing up there singing in front of everyone!'

'You looked lovely!' insisted Charlotte. 'Really you did, and your singing was breathtaking–'

'Quite the voice of an angel!' put in Andrew softly, coming to stand at Charlotte's side. 'The evening was an enormous success, thanks in no small measure to your vocal contribution, Miss Burdon.'

'You're very gracious, Mr Holcomb.' She blushed prettily. 'Charlotte, are you coming now? Mother is taking your parents home to the parsonage in our carriage.'

Charlotte shook her head, returning the

smile. 'I'm staying a little longer to help Hester with the clearing-up. Goodnight, Sophy – my word, it's past midnight! Christmas Eve already!'

She found Hester coming downstairs after seeing Captain Holcomb to his bed.

'I expect the Captain is worn out, but he looked very happy, didn't he?'

'I've never seen him looking so proud! Andrew really excelled himself as host, didn't he? I'll just make Father's hot toddy and take it up,' said Hester cheerily, fetching rum and dark brown sugar for the Captain's nightcap. 'Thank you again for all you've done, Charlotte.'

With Hester upstairs at the far end of the house, Gaw Hill fell silent except for the muffled clatter from the kitchen, and Charlotte was snuffing out the last of the dining-room candles when raised voices erupted from the library.

Alarmed, she swept across the hall and burst into the room.

'–it's beyond belief, man!' Will was declaring furiously. 'What do you reckon you're playing at?'

'That's hardly your concern, is it?' replied Andrew, splashing more whisky into his glass. 'Or is that what galls you?'

'It's to do with this family and that *makes* it my concern!' retaliated Will. 'For I care what happens to folk, even if you don't give a tuppenny–'

'Enough!' hissed Charlotte, closing the door firmly behind her and rounding on both men, eyes blazing. 'It's past midnight – it's Christmas Eve, for heaven's sake! – shout any louder and you'll rouse the entire household.'

'Keep out of this, Lottie,' muttered Andrew, turning to pour another drink, his words slurring slightly. 'This is between Will and I.'

'Do you really want your father and Hester to hear you quarrelling?' she challenged. 'Can't you at least keep your differences to yourselves? Or are you both so selfish you want to spoil what's been a lovely evening for them both?'

Will glowered across the library at Andrew, but was first to acquiesce.

'I've said my piece – for tonight – but I'll not let this go, Andrew. You'll not get away with it, I'll see to that!'

Andrew completely ignored his boyhood friend, inclining his head in deference to Charlotte. 'You are quite right as usual, Lottie. I apologise for our appalling behaviour. Will, your comments are well-meant I am sure. We will, as you suggest, discuss this further upon a more appropriate occasion.'

'You know your trouble, Andrew? You get everything handed to you on a plate and you care for nobody but yourself,' Will said evenly, starting from the library. 'You're abusing folks' trust. Worse than that, you're dishonest and disloyal to–'

'Will, that's not fair!' cried Charlotte impulsively. 'Whatever disagreements you and Andrew may have, those are dreadful charges! Andrew is taking care of everything in his own way!'

'Andrew will always do things his own way until the day of reckoning,' went on Will sarcastically. 'Then you don't see him for dust, just like four years ago–'

'The past is the past,' interrupted Charlotte hotly. 'Andrew didn't want to leave Hild Head – he told me so – it was his father and Hester who made him go–'

Andrew had taken his glass and had stretched out in a fireside chair, merely a spectator upon events, his expressionless gaze lingering upon Charlotte's flushed face.

'You know nowt about it, Charlotte,' snapped Will.

He wasn't looking at her. His grey eyes were narrowed, never once leaving Andrew's face as he watched him watching Charlotte.

'I'm warning you, Andrew – I'll not let you get away with this!'

'Is that right?' Andrew enquired lazily.

Then he waved a dismissive hand.

'No matter. Bring the carriage around. It's time Charlotte went home.'

Without another word, Will strode from the library and Charlotte half expected the door to slam behind him, but he held it fast until it closed.

Suddenly she and Andrew were alone and she realised she was trembling.

'Whatever's going on?' she mumbled unsteadily, going to him and dropping to her knees at the side of his chair. 'I've never ever seen the two of you like that.'

He shrugged, touching a hand to the smoothness of her hair. 'Will and I have had disagreements in the past.'

'Disagreements, yes, but this ... such terrible anger and bitterness!' She shook her head sadly. 'You and Will, you were closer than many brothers!'

'Brothers fight, Lottie.' He poured another drink and replaced the crystal stopper in the decanter with a clink. 'Remember your Bible!'

'It's about more than your taking over the

Holcomb Line, isn't it?' she persisted. 'What has gone so very badly wrong between you?'

'With Will and I? Can you really not guess, Lottie?' He allowed her name to linger on his tongue before swallowing the last of his whisky and then drew her from her knees, up on to his lap and into his arms, tightening his embrace and claiming her lips with a bruising kiss.

When finally he let her go, Charlotte staggered backwards, her knees weak.

Turning, she saw the library door that had been closed was now ajar, and sensed rather than knew that Will had entered the room and left again silently.

Andrew was pulling her close again, catching both her hands. 'Come awhile to the fireside before you go home, Lottie...'

'Excuse me, please, a moment–' she stammered, pulling free and hurrying from the library, shutting the door behind her.

She sped along the hall, her heart thumping, looking in through open doors as she went. Each room was quite empty. Doubling back along the hall, she went outdoors.

A lantern burned in the stable, and she could see the silhouette of the horse and carriage harnessed and waiting. Then she realised Will was there, too. He heard her footsteps and turned around.

'Carriage is ready,' he said indifferently. 'Is Andrew driving you, or does he want me to do it?'

'Will, what you saw in the–'

'Like Andrew said, what he does is none of my business.'

She accepted the unspoken rebuke, and went on. 'You're annoyed with me, aren't you? Because I took Andrew's part in the argument?'

'The argument?' he echoed stonily. 'No, Charlotte. I'm not annoyed with you. As for taking his side, well, you speak as you feel. That's fair enough.'

'But you're upset and hurt, Will! I can't bear it when–' she reached out to touch his arm, but he shook her off as though branded with a smoking iron.

'Don't Charlotte – just *don't!*'

'Please don't push me away, Will–'

'Lottie!' the shout and approaching footsteps came from across the yard. 'Are you out there...?'

'Go, Charlotte! For pity's sake, just go back to Andrew before – go to Andrew.' Will turned from her, his voice thick. 'He's the one you love. Lord help you, you just can't see beyond the swagger and the pretty words, can you?'

In the seconds before Andrew Holcomb strode into the cobbled yard, Will swung around, gripping Charlotte's shoulders so fiercely she cried out.

'Words and charm are all there is with him,' he said through clenched teeth. 'Be warned, he'll take you and your heart and whatever else he wants, but Andrew'll not wed you, lass – never in a million years!'

Tragedy Strikes!

The New Year came in grey and bitterly cold and, during the early weeks of January, vessels in Whitby's harbour battened down against the gale-force easterly winds sweeping in from the German Ocean.

Tucked away from the waterfront, midway along the genteel shopping street of Bishopsgate, soft light gleamed in the small panes of the milliner's window, brightening the dreary winter morning.

'You're making a nice job of that,' Madge Prentise was saying, watching as Charlotte arranged hats on a stand before an oval mirror. 'If that new window display of yours doesn't bring stampedes of ladies through our door, nothing will!'

Charlotte laughed. She'd grown fond of her forthright employer during the time she'd been working at the hat shop.

'I hope you're right – we've been very quiet these past weeks!'

'It's this stormy weather. It puts the ladies off going out because they get the hems of

124

their frocks wet,' commented Madge, adding, 'I'll be sorry to lose you when my niece gets back from Leeds. You've a nice way with the customers – comes from being a clergyman's daughter, I expect! When's your ma leaving to visit your sister?'

'Not for another month or so. Will says the road into the Lakes often gets snowbound well past Easter, but Ma's hoping to get there in plenty of time so she can help Lucy with Bea and the house.'

Madge nodded. 'And have you got all you wanted for your ma's trip?'

Charlotte nodded, her smile widening. Madge knew all about her saving-up.

'I've already given Ma the boots, it seemed silly to have them wrapped up and hidden away when she might be wearing them and keeping warm, and Bessie and I have nearly finished making her coat, so she'll have that for the journey. It'll take more than a day and a half, apparently. And that's if none of the roads are closed by rain or snow.'

'It's the mail coach she's going on, isn't it? They're the fastest and usually the most reliable – the driver gets fined if there are delays,' remarked Madge, glancing up from tidying a box of trimmings. 'I've been thinking, why don't you choose a nice bonnet for her to wear to the christening? Sort of a leaving present from me to you, for you're the best assistant I've had in a fair while – only don't let on to my niece about that, eh?'

'Thank you so much, Madge!' exclaimed Charlotte. 'Ma will be delighted – I can't remember her ever having a pretty bonnet!'

'You choose an extra nice one for her. Now, how about a pot of tea? I'll put the kettle on and you go across to the coffee house and fetch pastries – if we're to have a quiet day, we might as well make the most of it!'

Wrapping her cloak tightly about her, Charlotte sped along Bishopsgate to the Viennese coffee house where the appealing aroma of fresh-ground coffee mingled with the delicate fragrances of candied fruits and sweet spices, and small, circular tables set with crisp linen and fine porcelain were arranged around the room, each lit with a flickering fluted lamp, lending an air of intimacy.

Charlotte was standing waiting for her order to be prepared, when she began to feel distinctly uneasy – as though someone was *watching* her.

Turning sharply, she glanced over her shoulder and instantly met the gaze of Sophy

Burdon, who immediately averted her eyes to study the table linen.

Sophy was seated at a table tucked away in a corner alcove, and at her side was a young man in a high collar whom Charlotte did not recognise.

Instinctively, she glanced about the coffee house for the presence of Mrs Burdon or Sophy's younger sisters, but there was no sign of any of them.

'Your pastries, Miss Vale,' announced Mr Werner, brandishing the box of delicacies with a flourish. 'Enjoy! And please do offer my most gracious regards to Mrs Prentise.'

'I'll be sure to do so, Mr Werner,' replied Charlotte, suddenly aware that she'd been staring at Sophy and her companion. 'Thank you, and good day.'

Without another glance at the corner table, she quit the coffee house and, with head bowed against the cutting wind, hurried back along Bishopsgate.

Once back inside the milliner's, she and Madge Prentise had no sooner settled themselves in the cosy back room with their tea and pastries, than the tiny bell above the shop's door jingled.

'Isn't it always the way!' groaned Madge,

getting up and shaking her head at Charlotte, who had also risen. 'You finish your cake, I'll see to it.'

She stepped out into the shop to greet an agitated young lady.

'Miss Burdon! How nice to see you!' began Madge with a formal smile. 'How may we help you today?'

'Actually,' Sophy cleared her throat. 'I wondered if I might have a private word with Charlotte – Miss Vale?'

'Certainly, Miss Burdon,' replied Madge, discreetly withdrawing to the back room where Charlotte was finishing her apple strudel. 'It's Mrs Burdon's eldest!' she hissed. 'For you!'

Customers rarely asked especially for her, and Charlotte was completely unprepared for Sophy's reaction when she went out into the shop.

'Miss Vale – Charlotte–!' Sophy clutched her arm, pulling her to the furthest corner where there was least chance of their conversation being overheard in the back room. 'I must speak with you! About – about what you saw in the Viennese coffee house.'

'Sophy, calm yourself!' murmured Charlotte. 'I thought little of seeing you and had almost forgotten about it.'

'Oh, if only you would!' she cried. 'Come to tea and we'll find a moment to talk privately – it's of the utmost importance!'

'I'm sorry, Sophy, but I'll be here until long after tea time and then there are parish visits that I must make this evening.'

'In that case I will tell Mother that I'm to accompany you on your visits. She'll approve of that and won't ask awkward questions. I'll bring the gig and await you at The Bear. At what hour will you come?'

An arrangement was made and, as the two girls parted, Sophy clasped both Charlotte's hands. 'Until this evening then. And, promise me, you won't breathe a word to anyone – about anything!'

It was a long, bitterly cold walk that evening, away from the lights of Whitby old town and up along the windswept cliff path away to Hild Head.

Charlotte was weary and chilled to the bone, and darkness had long since fallen before she reached the village, at once seeing the Burdons' gig outside The Old White Bear.

Sophy must have been watching from a window within for, as Charlotte drew near, she appeared from the ladies' parlour.

'Come inside,' she urged. 'We'll be quite alone and can speak freely!'

'I cannot tarry,' returned Charlotte crisply. 'If you wish to talk, you must do so as we walk. I have several folk to visit.'

Sophy frowned, then sighed. 'Very well. But we will not walk. I shall drive you wherever you're going.' She climbed into the gig and settled herself inside. 'This is altogether very distressing for me, Charlotte.'

'Can you not just tell me whatever it is that troubles you?' Charlotte tried not to allow impatience into her voice as she clambered up into the gig.

'You've kept your promise?' persisted Sophy, snapping the reins so that the horse moved off briskly along the rutted street. 'You truly haven't told a soul about seeing me in the coffee house this afternoon? And you must give your solemn word you will not repeat what I am about to tell you?'

'I'll naturally honour any confidence,' responded Charlotte, rubbing her cold fingers vigorously to ease their numbness. 'But why do you feel compelled to confide in me at all?'

'I have no choice,' returned Sophy bleakly, her eyes looking straight ahead as the gig travelled away from the village and up towards Trimmel Bank. 'The young man you saw me with is very dear to me. His name is Ralph Kirrige and he is a clerk at Whitehead's Bank in the old town. It was at the bank we met, while I was there with Mama. Ralph and I met again, quite by chance, when my sisters and I were in the bookseller's before Christmas. Ralph and I have been... We've been meeting secretly ever since.'

'Why? Doesn't your mother like him?' Charlotte asked sympathetically.

'Mama doesn't *know* about him– Nor must she!'

'Why not? If he is as nice as you say–'

'You just don't understand! *You* can wander about meeting people and doing things and nobody turns a hair, but it's different for someone like me! It just isn't proper for an unmarried young *lady* to behave so,' she cut in agitatedly. 'But Ralph is a fine man and oh, he does so warm my heart!'

'Then you cannot keep him a secret from your mother,' remarked Charlotte evenly. 'Not if you and he are to share a future together.'

'That's the whole point, we *have* no future because Ralph doesn't have any money!' she cried. 'I'm sure one day he *will* be wealthy, for he is clever and ambitious and Josiah

Whitehead, the owner of the bank, regards him very highly, but Mama would never countenance a penniless suitor! Should she discover we're meeting, she'll forbid me ever to see him again.'

'This is your private family business,' murmured Charlotte uncomfortably. It's–'

'You don't know anything about my family, do you?' cut in Sophy.

'Not really,' admitted Charlotte. She knew the Burdons from church, of course, but they had never visited the parsonage and the Vales hadn't been invited to their home on The Crescent.

'We're as poor as church mice!' announced Sophy, urging the horse to go faster. 'You wouldn't believe how hard-up we are.'

Charlotte said nothing at first, gazing ahead through the night and considering the parishioners who were patiently waiting for her visit.

'Don't you have a big house somewhere in Wharfedale?'

'Egleton. But how naïve you are! Yes, we have a big house – a big house that is more burden than benefit! Henry VII granted the manor of Egleton to the Burdons in the 1500s, and we still have the land and the Hall of course, but it's in a dreadful state.

Grandfather wasn't very good at managing the estate and poor Papa was hopeless about money, so when he died ... there is a caretaker at the estate now, but it's mostly all left to ruin,' she concluded dismally. 'We had to sell Mother's jewellery and all sorts of things just to move here. The house on The Crescent belongs to family friends. It isn't ours.'

'Couldn't you sell your house at Egleton?'

'Selling our family seat would be unthinkable,' she answered curtly. 'And since we can't afford to stock and manage the estate ourselves, Mama is determined I marry a rich husband to bring money back into the family.'

'But you love Ralph!'

'That would be of no concern to Mama!' snorted Sophy. 'Although I don't see why one of my sisters can't marry a rich man – when they're old enough – and have Egleton. I don't want it. I just want Ralph.'

'But you can't go on meeting in secret forever! What are you going to do?'

'I don't know!' cried Sophy miserably. 'I don't care what I have to do so long as I have Ralph – I'll do anything on this earth to keep him!'

On Charlotte's final day at the millinery, she

and Madge Prentise devoted much time to choosing a hat for Edith Vale.

'Finer bonnets you'll not see anywhere, even if I do say so myself!' declared Madge, selecting a neat, wide-brimmed hat. 'You said pink was your mam's favourite colour? This one is a lovely shade of rose, and you could make it a bit more special for the christening by trimming it with these little flowers. Here, take 'em outside into the daylight and see how the colours match before you decide.'

Carefully taking the bonnet and spray of delicate silk flowers, Charlotte stepped outside into the busy street and held one against the other.

Madge had an experienced eye, and the subtle colours complimented each other perfectly, making the modest bonnet very pretty and feminine.

Pleased, Charlotte turned back towards the shop, but froze as she saw the foreigner from the Black Jack Tavern striding along the opposite pavement, deep in conversation with a tall man walking at his side.

Charlotte scurried back inside and all but slammed the door behind her.

'What's up with you? You look like you've seen a–'

'Madge, quickly!' She gripped the other woman's arm and tugged her to the window. 'Do you know who that man is? Over there, by the matchgirl?'

'The incredibly handsome, well-dressed gent?' enquired Madge, describing Andrew Holcomb. 'Never seen him before – I wish I had! Why?'

'Not him! The other one!'

'Oh, I know *him* all right! Or at least, I know *of* him.' She sniffed disdainfully. 'He's famous – *infamous*, more like – here in the old town. Passes himself off as a Portuguese gentleman but he's the biggest villain this side of the hangman's gibbet! Goes by the name of Cristiano Maias although, if half I've heard is true, that's probably not his right name!'

'Who is he?' went on Charlotte, turning from the window now that both men had disappeared into the crowd. 'I mean, what does he do? How would a – a gentleman come to know him?'

Madge pursed her lips, lowering her voice even though the two women were alone in the shop.

'Maias owns the Black Jack Tavern on Jericho Street down by the waterfront. You won't know of it. It's a low place, but there's

135

many a gent goes in there through a private door. The Black Jack's a den of vice. Strong liquor, gambling. Opium. All sorts goes on there. It's nothing short of a bawdy house. And that's probably not the worst of it.'

Charlotte stared at her. Surely, there must be some reasonable explanation why Andrew would have anything to do with such a man. Or such a place.

'Maybe you're mistaken, Madge,' she suggested. 'I mean, there's often not a grain of truth to gossip.'

'True enough, but there's no smoke without fire, either. A young lass got murdered at the Black Jack some years back,' commented Madge with a sharp dip of her chin. 'Didn't cause much of a stir at first, then there was talk the girl belonged to some well-to-do family from miles away and had somehow been *sold* to Maias. 'Course, it was all hushed up and nothing more was ever heard. A man like Maias has important friends in high places. He can pull more strings in this town than a puppeteer! The least you know about his sort, Charlotte, the better,' concluded Madge, lining a hat box with soft paper. 'So, have you decided on this rose bonnet for your mam? It's a beautiful one, and the spray of flowers just sets it off, doesn't it?'

Charlotte and Madge Prentise said their farewells at the end of that day. 'You be sure to come back and visit,' insisted Madge. 'We'll have a cup of tea, a couple of Mr Werner's pastries and a good old natter! Remember me to your mama!'

Carefully carrying the box containing Ma's bonnet, Charlotte went from the millinery out on to Bishopsgate, her gaze fixed upon the opposite pavement where just a few hours earlier she had seen Andrew deep in conversation with the notorious Portuguese.

Did the dreadful tales Madge related have any substance? Had some poor unfortunate girl indeed been murdered–

'Charlotte!' Andrew was suddenly at her side, jarring her from the depths of her troubled thoughts. 'I'm sorry I'm a little late meeting you. Was this really your last day at that ghastly shop?'

'I wish it were not,' she responded absently, her mind still much distracted.

He took her arm, slipping it through his own and they started along the broad curve of Bishopsgate. Moments later, he swept her from the cold darkness of the crowded street into the enveloping warmth of the coffee house.

Her gaze darted to the secluded alcove where she had witnessed Sophy Burdon with her young man – and was astonished to see them there again!

A quick glance up at Andrew assured her he had not noticed the couple seated in the discreet corner.

'May we sit over there, by the window?' she asked, indicating a table from which Sophy and Ralph Kirrige would not be visible.

'Wherever you please.' Andrew smiled as they took their seats. 'You'll have heard of the annual ball given to honour Whitby's great and good – not to mention the just plain rich and utterly unscrupulous?'

'Hester was telling me about it while we were cleaning the church together. She said Captain Holcomb is immensely proud that you are to represent the family and the Holcomb Line at the ball this year–' she broke off, looking sharply at him. 'Andrew, you *are* going to attend, aren't you?'

'Only if you accompany me,' he replied, sipping the fragrant coffee that Frederick Werner had brought to their table.

'Oh, no! No. You must go with Hester.

That's right and proper,' relied Charlotte firmly. 'Besides, I've never been anywhere so grand. I'd be completely out of my depth.'

He sliced into his kirsch torte with a gleaming silver fork. 'Well, if I cannot escort the lady of my choice, I shan't go either. I've precious little interest as it is in these parochial affairs that appear so important to my father and sister.'

'But the Captain and Hester will be bitterly disappointed!' she exclaimed in consternation. 'You have to go, Andrew! The ball may mean nothing to you, but would it really be so very difficult for you to attend for their sake?'

He grinned wryly at her, his dark eyes sparkling.

'You do realise I could just as neatly turn around that argument and demand the same of you?'

'You need say no more,' she murmured, surveying him above the rim of her coffee cup. 'I'll primp and pin up my hair and come with you.'

'Thank you, Lottie.' He reached out to cover her small hand with his own. 'You will be the most beautiful lady there, and I the proudest and most fortunate of men.'

She lowered her eyes, a frown troubling

her forehead.

'Andrew,' she began, no longer able to contain that which had troubled her all day long. 'The Portuguese who accosted us outside the Crown Buildings; who *is* he?'

'Which man?' queried Andrew irritably.

'His name is Cristiano Maias,' she persisted doggedly, but stopped short of actually mentioning having witnessed Andrew in his company on more than one occasion. I – I've seen him around the town.'

'He hasn't bothered you, has he?'

'Of course not. Why would he?'

'There are all manner of dangers in a busy port like Whitby,' he went on gravely, his eyes concerned as he looked upon her. 'Dangers you cannot even imagine – I don't like you venturing alone into town. You must promise me to be constantly vigilant?' Then he changed the topic entirely.

However Charlotte heard not a word of his conversation, for her mind was preoccupied with the turmoil of her thoughts.

What threat did Andrew perceive the Portuguese posed to her? Why had he not simply admitted knowing Cristiano Maias? Was he so deeply ashamed of his association with such a man that he could not bear to confess it?

Why hadn't he told her the truth?

Charlotte finished the chapter of the book she was reading aloud to Widow Tunstall, and made a fresh pot of tea for the elderly woman before taking her leave and setting off to meet Will down in the village.

They were to go up to Peterson's mill to fetch flour.

The clock of St Hild's was striking the quarter hour by the time Charlotte came within sight of The Old White Bear, and when Snuffy saw Will waiting there, she immediately raced off and was already up on the seat when Charlotte reached the wagon.

'How is Captain Holcomb?' she asked at once, taking Will's hand and clambering up. 'Is his cold any better?'

'Aye, much.' Jiggling the reins, he guided the sturdy pony through the village and out toward the cliff path.

'Master's on the mend and shouting the odds, but even a year ago, he'd have taken a cold like this in his stride, but now...'

His gaze darted sidelong and met hers.

'He doesn't have the strength to fight any more, Charlotte. Least thing lays him low and leaves him weak as a bairn.'

'Oh, Will! You're really worried about him,

141

aren't you?'

Instinctively she squeezed the rough hand holding the reins, then seeing Will's glance fall to their joined hands, let go her gentle touch and almost whispered.

'I'm so very sorry.'

'Are you?' he demanded, facing her now. His grey eyes, darker than gritstone and just as hard, bored into her. 'About what, exactly? – Ah, never mind! What difference does it make?'

He turned from her, staring at the steep, rocky road ahead.

'I – I don't understand...'

'No, happen you don't at that. Why should you?'

He expelled a ragged breath, drawing the wagon in close to one side of the uneven mill track so that a woman and her young son might pass easily with the makeshift cart they were dragging behind them.

'You're going to the February Ball this Friday, so Andrew tells me?'

'I'm sure it will be very grand,' she responded, and her thrill of anticipation had less to do with the occasion than with the prospect of spending an entire evening with Andrew.

'It matters a great deal to Captain Holcomb and Hester that the family be represented at the ball, although Andrew wasn't at all keen to go.'

'Was he not?' enquired Will dryly. 'Fancy! That's not how I heard it! It's a grand do, isn't it? All those rich and powerful folk rubbing shoulders and brokering deals? Just the place for him to be seen by them as count for something.'

Not another word passed between the old friends for the rest of the journey. Presently, the mill came into view and Will sprang down. The windmill was placed on high ground, taking the full weight of the offshore winds tearing in across the German Ocean.

'You stay put; I'll fetch the sacks.'

The drive home passed with their exchanging the occasional comment but never really talking.

For several weeks now, Charlotte had wanted to ask Will about Cristiano Maias, but as the distance between them increased, so did the notion of disloyalty to Andrew if she discussed such matters. Once, it would have been the most natural thing to voice concern about one friend to the other.

As they approached the parsonage, they both noticed the Burdons' gig outside St Hild's, the horse standing in the full force of the east wind.

'Why folk can't have a care, I'll never know!' muttered Will, drawing the wagon to a standstill and jumping down. 'I'll move him into the shelter of the gorse–'

He was no sooner leading the horse away than a young woman ran from the church porch and down the winding path, hailing Charlotte.

'I called at the parsonage but your maid said you were out for the afternoon,' she began, without a glance to Will as he tended to her horse and gig. 'I've been sitting in the porch waiting!'

'Why didn't you wait at the parsonage?' enquired Charlotte. 'Come indoors–'

'I can't!' she hissed, glancing towards Will. 'I have to see you alone!'

Will certainly could not have overheard the exchange. However, he nonetheless appeared to gain the gist of what was being said for, as he started back towards the laden wagon, he glanced at Charlotte.

'Happen I'll go on up and unload the sacks,' he commented. 'In the larder as usual, is it?'

'Yes, thank you, Will.'

'The church, Charlotte– We may talk there!' insisted Sophy, drawing her compan-

144

ion hurriedly up the path and into St Hild's. 'Something quite dreadful has happened! You must help me!'

'Of course I'll help, if I can.' Charlotte urged Sophy to sit and calm herself. 'Whatever is wrong?'

'It's Ralph!' Sophy cried, her cheeks flushed. 'Mama was to be at the Bible Society today, so I slipped away from The Crescent and into town to meet him. But when I returned home, Mama was already there and waiting for me! Her meeting had ended early and she demanded to know where I had been and what I had been doing out alone for so many hours – so I told her I'd been with you!'

'You told her *what?*' demanded Charlotte in horror. 'You *lied* to your mother?'

'What choice did I have? If Mama discovers the truth, she'll forbid me to see Ralph. I said you and I had done some dusting here at St Hild's and then I'd accompanied you on your parish rounds. I knew she'd approve of that. So, if she asks – and I'm certain she won't – she only ever sees you in church on Sundays, after all – but if she should mention it, you won't give me away, will you?'

Charlotte stared at her in disbelief. 'Sophy, this is wrong!'

'It's easy for you to be self-righteous! You can't imagine what my life is like!' snapped Sophy. 'You're free to come and go and do as you please! Mama will force me into marriage with anybody who's sufficiently wealthy. Although we're still in mourning, she's been discreetly searching for suitors since we came here. There are many rich men in a prosperous town like Whitby, and it won't matter a jot how old or fat or disgusting he is!'

'If your mother asks me outright, then I must tell her the truth,' responded Charlotte at length. 'Otherwise, I'll keep your secret.'

'Bless you!' Sophy kissed her upon both cheeks, her tears transformed into smiles. 'I love Ralph so – I couldn't bear to lose him!'

In a flurry of satin and merino, Sophy swept from the church to her waiting gig, leaving Charlotte alone in the half-light.

'What's up with Miss Burdon?' The west door opened and Will stepped inside, his soft voice echoing in the empty church. 'I've just seen her driving away like a bat out of – like the devil himself were after her. I didn't realise you and her were friends.'

'We're not friends!' replied Charlotte with feeling, immediately apologetic. 'Sorry, Will.

I didn't mean to bite your head off. It's just that... I really don't know Sophy. Until recently, when I saw her by chance in Whitby, we'd never even spoken to each other properly, except for being polite after church.'

'Friendships can grow from unlikely beginnings,' remarked Will, walking with her up to the parsonage. 'Myself, I can't imagine two lasses with less in common than you and Sophy Burdon, but that don't mean you can't be friends.'

'Mean spirited as it sounds, I fear Sophy seeks me out only when she needs a favour,' murmured Charlotte. 'She's in an awkward situation and I do sympathise with her, but what she asks me to do is... Well, it's not straightforward.'

'Then you must do what you believe is right.' He pushed open the gate, standing aside for her to enter. 'In you go. You're shivering and Bessie's near ready to dish up.'

'Will you stay and eat with us?' she asked him quietly. 'It seems such a long while since you spent an evening with us.'

'Thanks, but no. I've got to get back to Gaw Hill,' he replied with something of their old easiness. 'There are a few chores Andrew wants done before he gets home from

Whitby, tonight, so I'd best make tracks.'

She left him at the gate, watching until he'd returned to the wagon before going indoors herself.

Shedding her coat and muddy boots in the passage, she padded in her stockinged feet through to the kitchen and was met by the mouth-watering aroma of hotpot and fresh bread.

Bessie Proud glanced over her shoulder. 'It'll be on the table and going cold by the clock's strike– If you hurry, you'll just have time to open your box.'

'What box?'

'The big, striped box the delivery boy from a fancy shop in Whitby brought up here at dinner time,' replied Bessie matter-of-factly. 'The same box I put in your room to wait for you!'

With Snuffy clattering at her heels, Charlotte raced upstairs and into her room.

A long, deep box from Whitby's finest dressmaker lay upon her quilt. Her fingers trembled as she pulled away the ribbons and raised the lid to reveal the most exquisite gown she'd ever set eyes upon.

The shining satin skirts tumbled in pools and waves of turquoise and silver, the bodice ruched and beaded.

148

There were matching gloves and satin dancing slippers too, and an ornament for her hair.

Tears of surprise and delight filled her eyes; however, it was not the lavish gift nor even the kind gesture that moved her so, but the small card bearing the simple words written in a dear, fluent hand.

With love, Andrew.

Despite having had the latest of nights, with everyone in the parsonage being long abed when Andrew drove her home from the February Ball, Charlotte was wide awake and up even earlier than usual the following morning.

It was a cold, clear morning with the shimmer and sparkle of a hard frost and, walking Snuffy briskly along the sand, Charlotte was in a dream as she recalled the gaiety and grandeur of the ball, and the sheer wonder of being in Andrew's arms as they danced and danced.

The rising winter sun was flushing her cheeks as she returned to the parsonage, her memory lingering upon those final few moments when he'd delivered her home, kissing her so very slowly and deeply until her every nerve was taut and tingling from the sensation of his caress.

Unable to contain her happiness, she broke into a run and sped the remaining distance along the cliff path, bursting into the parsonage just as Jacob Vale was emerging from his study.

'I expected you to be a sluggerbed today.' He beamed at her over his spectacles. 'Seeing as how you were out dancing and making merry long after sensible folk were asleep in their beds.'

'Oh, it was the most wonderful night, Pa!' she exclaimed, her face wreathed in smiles. 'Everything was just perfect– Why are you wearing your best collar and waistcoat?'

'I'm invited to luncheon with the vicar of St Mary's, so I'm off into town this morning,' he replied, admiring his reflection in the hall glass. 'I realise such an occasion doesn't nearly match up to Whitby's February Ball for grandness, but it's the best a poor country parson can hope for.'

'I'll walk with you,' said Charlotte at once. 'I can visit Madge Prentise and tell her all about the ball, I promised I would!'

Later that morning, Charlotte and her father set off upon the long walk along the cliff path towards the old town. Charlotte's boots rang upon the frosty stones and cracked the frozen puddles and ruts.

'I'm glad you enjoyed the dancing,' Jacob was saying, puffing his pipe into smoky plumes as they walked in the crisp air. 'And the company of a certain young man!'

Charlotte blushed.

'Your ma and I never imagined Andrew would be the one for you,' he mused. 'We always thought– Ah, but love has a funny old way of turning everything on its ear! He's a fine man, and Samuel has told me how pleased he is that Andrew's taken to running the company like a duck to water.'

'I just feel so happy, Pa! I feel like smiling all the time!'

'I'll let you into a secret. Even after so many years, sometimes I'll be all alone and I still can't help smiling when I think of your ma and know I'll be seeing her soon!'

Fog was drifting in from the German Ocean and the red-tiled roofs of the old town became blurred with wraiths of shifting mist. Chill dampness clung to Charlotte's hair and clothing, settling upon the icy path in a sheen of slippery moisture beneath their feet as father and daughter walked together.

'Poor Pa!' she murmured. 'You must be dreading Ma's going away.'

'Don't you let on now! But, aye. I'll miss her something terrible. We've never been apart before. Not once since we married. I can't imagine a day passing without seeing Edie's dear face or hearing her voice.'

'Just last week, Ma was saying the exact same thing!' exclaimed Charlotte. 'Only *she* didn't want *you* to know how sorely she'll miss you!'

Jacob turned away, blowing his nose into a huge white handkerchief.

'Your ma and me are a right pair and no mistake!' He turned towards his daughter and smiled, his eyes watery. 'I'm looking forward to giving her that fancy Easter bonnet, I want to see her in it before she leaves. You're sure she won't find it?'

'Absolutely certain! It's hidden somewhere she'll never look!'

Slipping her arm through his, Charlotte and her father walked briskly, their footsteps ringing and their breath billowing upon the cold air.

'I'll come down into the town with you,' Jacob remarked. 'I want to collect a couple of things from the bookseller before I go up to St Mary's. You be sure to have a nice day with Madge, and thank her again from me for your ma's rosy bonnet.'

'I will. We've a lot to catch up on– We're going to have pastries and a good chat!'

'Sounds much livelier than my luncheon with the vicar and the bishop, but I suppose I mustn't grumble.' He beamed at her over his spectacles. 'I'll see you this evening– Your ma was baking plum crumble when we came out, so I won't be late home!'

They parted at Bishopsgate, Charlotte continuing along the busy thoroughfare, while Jacob paused at the brewery corner to cross over into the narrow, winding little close where the bookseller had his premises.

Charlotte quickened her step, eager to tell Madge all about the ball.

Passing the Viennese coffee house, she looked back to wave to her father, but Jacob didn't see her. He was still standing patiently on the busy corner, waiting while a heavily laden dray manoeuvred out from the brewery yard.

As if in slow motion, Charlotte saw the dray's wheels lose their purchase on the icy cobbles and the huge wagon overturning, taking the heavy horse down with it and throwing the driver from his seat.

Casks burst free of their ropes, crashing down and splitting wide open.

Cries rang out from the onlookers as wine

and beer flowed like blood over the road and into the gutters.

'Pa!' The anguished cry rose to Charlotte's lips, but no sound came as she tried in vain to shout.

Pushing through the gathering crush of people, and skidding across the treacherous wet ice, she dropped to her knees beside the broken figure lying still and lifeless on the sparkling cobbles, the fallen casks all about him.

'Oh, *Pa!*'

Betrayal!

Pulling her cloak tight about her, Charlotte slipped from the unlit parsonage with a subdued Snuffy padding at her side.

It was barely dawn, and Ma's daffodils were in full bloom and bright in the half-light. Noiselessly closing the front door behind her, she heard the rustle of movement nearby and a soft voice speaking her name.

Glancing around, she saw Will stiffly straightening up from where he'd been sitting, his back against the low garden wall. He looked chilled to the bone.

'I had an idea you might be up before first light this morning. I wanted to be here whenever you came out. How's your ma?'

'She was awake all night, but I looked in just now and she's sleeping at last.'

'Best thing for her, I reckon.' He fell into step beside her as they passed St Hild's. 'How are you doing, yourself?'

She cast a backward glance to the churchyard with its mound of freshly turned earth.

'Although Pa had died, it seemed like he

155

was still with us. But after yesterday...' Her voice trailed off.

Will and Andrew had been among the bearers who had carried Jacob Vale to his final rest and who had stood alongside Ma and herself while the final words were read.

She bowed her head, quickening her pace towards the cliff steps. 'Now he's really gone from us forever, isn't he? We never will...'

Great shuddering sobs racked her body, but her eyes remained dry.

Will hesitated a moment before enveloping her within his arms.

'Come here, lass! Cry it all out, Charlotte. Just cry it all out...'

Holding her tightly, he drew her down to sit on the rough steps.

Snuffy hovered unhappily, pushing with her soft nose at Charlotte's cold hands while her mistress wept, the hot tears flowing as if they might never cease.

At length, the sobs subsided and Charlotte recovered her composure, sitting hunched and weak, her face turned seawards to the distant tide, her head and shoulders leaning heavily against the coarse cloth of Will's coat as he held her.

'How long had you been outside the parsonage?' she mumbled at last.

He shrugged. 'A while.'

She twisted around to look up at him. 'Were you there all night, Will?'

He shrugged again, averting his eyes. 'I just wanted to be close by.'

'You're a good friend, Will,' she whispered, her gaze directed far across the ocean once more. 'The dearest friend.'

'It's not hard to be your friend, Charlotte. Nor to care about what happens to you,' he replied, adding roughly, 'We'd best make a move – this isn't giving Snuffs much of a walk!'

Rising, he took her hands and helped her down the steep steps on to the beach.

Despite the cold, they strolled, watching the vibrant colours of the breaking sunrise, following the flight of oyster catchers as they rose in a cloud from the wet sand and swirled away across the water before winging around again and settling as one upon another stretch of dark sand.

'During the night, I wrote to Lucy,' remarked Charlotte, her eyes on the fiery horizon. 'Told her everything about yesterday. She was dreadfully upset not to be able to come home to say goodbye to Pa.'

'In her condition, it would've been foolhardy. It's a long and arduous journey even in the best of weather and circumstances,' commented Will. 'If you give me the letter, I'll see it goes soonest.'

'Ma's talking about delaying her trip, but I don't want her to do that, Will.' She raised her earnest eyes to his. 'She must go as planned! Lucy is expecting her at the end of next week and besides, sending Ma on this trip meant so very much to Pa.'

'Aye, he told me all about it!' Will smiled sadly. 'By, it gave him such pleasure to be saving up for the trip! Keeping it all secret and planning to surprise her!'

Charlotte nodded, swallowing hard. 'The last thing we ever talked about was how much he'd miss Ma while she was away. And – and how much he was looking forward to seeing her in the rose bonnet–'

'You're right about her going to Lucy's as arranged,' Will put in quietly. 'What about you, though? It's going to be hard, Charlotte.'

'That's another reason I want Ma to go as planned. I don't want her here when the parsonage is being emptied out and Pa's belongings parcelled up.'

'It's as well she doesn't have to be part of that,' he agreed soberly. 'Will you follow your ma to Lucy's? And settle in Tarnwithe?'

'I don't see how I can. Lucy and James wrote asking us both to go and live with them, but it's not possible. Their house is a tiny quarryman's terraced cottage. There'll be room for Ma, but for me to go as well isn't practical.'

'Is it right you can't stay at the parsonage?'

'Oh, yes. It was only Pa's while he was vicar and will be needed for the new incumbent's accommodation when somebody else gets the charge. Bessie and I will do all the sorting and clearing out after Ma has left for the Lakes. I don't want her seeing her old home broken up and sold off,' said Charlotte steadily as they reached Jonas Rock and turned for the homeward walk back. 'I want Ma's last memory of the parsonage to be just as it always was during the many happy years she and Pa lived there together.'

That afternoon, Captain Holcomb and Hester called at the parsonage and Charlotte was taken aback at how gaunt and grief-stricken the elderly man appeared. He had been much affected by the sudden death of his old friend and chess partner and struggling to accept the loss of Jacob Vale seemed to be draining every last ounce of his strength and spirit.

After a quiet word with Hester, Charlotte took the opportunity to go from the parsonage to fulfil her parish rounds. In truth, she was greatly relieved when the last was done. Her father had been much loved and respected in Hild Head, and the heartfelt sympathies and condolences of his parishioners were very hard for her to hear without crumbling into weeping. However, she did not return directly to the parsonage, but began walking from the village towards Whitby.

Upon reaching the old town, she took a circuitous route and walked another half-mile to avoid passing the treacherous corner where Pa had died and, once at the millinery, Madge immediately bustled her into the little back room and sent her niece to fetch pastries while she put the kettle to boil.

'Oh, Madge!' confided Charlotte, leaning forward to warm her hands above the small fire's glowing coals. 'Soon, I won't have a home nor any occupation in the world. I need to find lodgings and work. I understand you can't take me back at the shop,' she went on quickly. 'But I wondered – hoped – you might know of another shop where I might find employment?'

Madge frowned as she stirred another spoon of sugar into her tea. 'For lodgings, that's easy enough. There are a couple of respectable establishments here in town that offer room and board for ladies only. But with you being a lady and all, work'll be harder to come by.'

'I don't mind what I do, Madge. I really don't,' insisted Charlotte. 'I just need to find something very, very soon. And I'll be grateful for the addresses of the lodging houses.'

'I'll write 'em down.'

Madge turned, rising to take the box of pastries her niece was bringing into the cosy room.

'And I'll keep my ears open and ask around town for any vacancies. You're a bright girl, Charlotte. Don't fret yourself. You'll get fixed up somewhere. Now, shall we tuck into these lemon cakes while they're still warm?'

'I can't believe I'll never see this old house again,' murmured Edith Vale, lingering in the parsonage study and touching a trembling hand to Jacob's silver-rimmed spectacles, left folded upon the open page of a book as if he might at any moment return and resume reading. 'Charlotte, I don't want to leave you here alone!'

'Lucy needs you, Ma, and will do so even more when the baby comes. Besides, since Captain Holcomb and Hester have offered me a home at Gaw Hill, you know I'll be safe and well.'

'The Holcombs have always been as dear as family to us.'

After another moment, Edith went from the study, pausing in the hall to take the hat box from the table there. 'When you see Mrs Prentise, be sure to tell her how much I appreciate the bonnet, won't you? It's quite the prettiest I ever saw, and I certainly never wore anything so fine.' She reached up to kiss her daughter's smooth cheek. 'Thank you for choosing it for me, love.'

'It seems so long ago now. Pa–' she broke off, biting her lip and forcing back sharp tears and the vivid memory of her father's saying how much he looked forward to seeing Edith in her fancy bonnet. 'Pa – he thought it was very pretty, too.'

'I wish he…' With a sigh, Edith left the sentence unspoken and took Charlotte into her arms. 'Don't come with me to the coach! I'd rather we said our goodbyes here, in our old home. I pray not too many months will pass before we meet again!'

'Goodbye, Ma!' Charlotte struggled to

keep her voice steady and her eyes dry as she stood on the parsonage doorstep with Snuffy, watching as Edith went down the path and closed the gate behind her before being helped by Andrew into the Holcombs' carriage.

'Give my love to Lucy and James and Bea – I'll write often!'

The mail coach north into the Lakes travelled by night and so left The Old White Bear in the early evening.

Although the days were lengthening now, it was already growing dark as Charlotte moved softly about the parsonage making lists. She was lighting a candle when hoof beats thudded along the cliff path and, darting to the window, she saw Andrew tethering Caesar at the gate.

'Did Ma get away safely?' She ran out to meet him, welcoming the comfort of his embrace as he drew her into his arms and bent to kiss her forehead.

'Very comfortably, I'd say,' he replied as they went indoors. 'A pleasant couple were travelling inside with her, and there were three others up on the roof – I don't envy them their journey north, for it's to be a cold night!'

'I hope it'll be a safe one!' frowned Charlotte anxiously. 'Aren't mail coaches in great danger of being attacked when they're crossing the moors?'

'Such tales are greatly exaggerated, Lottie,' he answered dismissively. 'I myself saw the guard tonight. He was well-armed with a blunderbuss and a brace of pistols. Even if an attacker survived being shot, he'd be tried on a capital charge and face the gallows. You have absolutely no cause for concern.'

'I'll still be glad for the news that Ma has arrived and is safe with Lucy,' she replied, then added as an afterthought, 'I'm sorry! I should have offered you tea. Or coffee?'

'No, nothing.'

He shook his head, watching with gathering irritation as Charlotte dipped her pen and continued moving about the parlour.

'What in heaven's name are you doing?'

'I'm told we need to make an inventory,' she said unemotionally. 'Some of our belongings are to be packed up and sent to Ma and Lucy. As for the rest, there are a few bits and pieces that Bessie is fond of and shall have as keepsakes of her time here with us. And Pa would've wanted Will to have his books, I'm sure. If there's anything you or

164

Hester and your father would like from the parsonage, you're very welcome. I thought perhaps to offer Pa's chess set to the Captain – they had so many happy hours playing together!'

'Yes. Yes, they did.' Andrew touched his fingertips to her cold cheek. 'I'm certain Father would appreciate that gesture. However, why are you making an inventory? Surely that's not necessary?'

'All that was in the parsonage when Pa and Ma came here, must remain for the use of the new incumbent,' she explained, bending once more to her script. 'Everything else must be removed. I've to make a list so it can all go for auction at The Bear early next month.'

'Auction?' he echoed, shaking his head in exasperation. 'Lottie, why do you not simply get Will to empty the parsonage for you? A few trips with the wagon, and everything that belonged to your family can be taken up to Gaw Hill and stored there for as long as you choose!'

'I have no purpose nor place for our old things any more. It is better they be put to good use by others than be packed away to moulder,' she returned practically. 'Besides, I intend sending the monies raised from the auction to Ma, so she might have at least some... I don't expect you to understand the fear of penury, but it is very real for many.'

'I was pretty near broke a couple of times in Carolina when the cards were against me, if that's what you mean!' he responded dryly, taking her pen and writing tablet from her and gently pulling her down on to the couch beside him. 'Lottie, I want you to pack a bag and come back to Gaw Hill with me. Hester has your rooms ready and is expecting you for dinner tonight.'

'Andrew,' she began sorrowfully. 'I'm not ready to move away from the parsonage. Not yet.'

'Why not, Lottie? Now your mother has left, make a clean break!' he urged softly, silencing her objections by placing a gentle fingertip on her parted lips. 'Besides, if you seriously believe I'm about to leave you here alone in this isolated house, you're very much mistaken! And you need not worry about anything; I shall take care of the auction for you.'

'No,' she replied sadly, rising from his side. 'No, I must do it, Andrew. All this plain, ordinary stuff was part of Ma and Pa's life together. Things they used every day and loved well. I *have* to do this myself!'

'Very well.' He stood before her, bending to touch her mouth with a tender kiss. 'But remember, my darling, Gaw Hill is where you belong now and where you always shall. Away and fetch your bag, so we might go home...'

Those first weeks at Gaw Hill passed with surprising swiftness and Charlotte kept busy, settling into a daily routine of assisting Hester within the household wherever she was able, and continuing with her parish rounds.

'I can't imagine why you've come to doubt the propriety of it,' Hester was saying, as they knelt weeding the flower beds bordering the glass doors into the morning-room. 'Many folk in Hild Head depend upon your pastoral visits for a variety of reasons. They'd be left either in practical difficulties, or lonely and isolated from the community, were your visits to cease.'

'Those were my feelings, Hester. I thought to continue until the new vicar is installed,' commented Charlotte, pausing to gaze thoughtfully across the neat lawns to where Will was digging in the hedged kitchen garden with Snuffy at his side. 'However, perhaps it is inappropriate for–'

'Has Andrew been trying to dissuade you from your parish work?' interrupted Hester bluntly, sitting back on her heels. 'I might have guessed my brother was behind your misgivings! You must not heed him, Charlotte.'

'Andrew *does* have a point, though. I'm no longer a daughter of the clergy, am I?'

'Does that preclude you from offering help and comfort to those in need?' challenged Hester. 'Andrew has always been strong-minded and utterly determined to have his own way in everything. He cares deeply for you, Charlotte, I do believe that. However, you must stand fast against his will or see your own spirit crushed underfoot as he presses to gain his way.'

'How melodramatic you sound!' exclaimed Charlotte with a smile.

'I daresay you're right,' conceded Hester, returning the younger woman's smile rue-fully. 'And perhaps I am too quick to criticise and judge him. But how I wish to be more involved with life, Charlotte! Not just with running the house here but with the Holcomb Line itself. I have helped to run the business in the past, as you know. And I was good at it, Charlotte! I was! Even Father said I had a quick brain and a sharp nose for

168

trade. He and I would talk for hours about our ships and their voyages.

'But since Andrew has taken over, he's shut me out completely. And Will, too. He won't discuss the company at all, nor answer the most innocent of questions. I also suspect that my brother tells Father only that which he wishes him to know.'

She rose stiffly, pushing her straw sun hat back on to her neck and looking across the terrace to where Captain Holcomb was sitting in his chair, drowsing with an open book on his lap.

'Naturally, Father takes his son's part. Say's I'm not to meddle and it's for Andrew to run the Holcomb Line as he sees fit. I fear that pride and hope for his only son clouds his perceptions–'

Hester broke off as the maid, Liddie, came out from the morning-room and tiptoed past the Captain into the garden. 'Letter just come for you, Miss Charlotte.' She bobbed a curtsey and offered the silver tray. 'And is there anything else for the postbag? It's to go soon.'

Charlotte took the letter, at once recognising Madge Prentise's hand. 'Erm, yes – I've a letter for Ma and Lucy. It's on the writing table in my room, Liddie.'

'I'll see to it, miss.' With another bob, Liddie crept back across the terrace and into the house.

Not without a little apprehension, Charlotte broke the seal and unfolded the letter, hastily scanning Madge's neat script and breaking into a wide smile.

'Hester, you recall my mentioning Madge Prentise has been looking out for employment for me? It seems Mr Zachariah Mylecraine, who is a draper on Bebb Street, is seeking *"a refined young woman for his muslins counter"*, and Madge has recommended me! I'm to visit his shop and see him tomorrow!'

'That's marvellous news, Charlotte! Your interview is sure to be successful.'

Neither of them had noticed Andrew striding across the lawn from the stables.

'What's all the excitement about?' He grinned, looking from one face to the other. 'You'll wake Father with such high spirits!'

'I've had good news – well, *hopeful* news, at least!' replied Charlotte, offering him Madge's letter.

He read quickly, passing back the letter in annoyance.

'The whole notion is preposterous!'

'Why so?' challenged Charlotte in surprise. 'Weeks ago when I mentioned Madge was seeking employment for me, you voiced not a single objection!'

'Because I didn't imagine the woman foolish enough to actually get you a job!' he returned tersely, shaking his head. 'It's absurd, Lottie. I won't allow it!'

'It's hardly for you to allow or disallow,' put in Hester quietly. 'It is Charlotte's decision entirely. If she wishes to proceed, then I believe it admirable.'

'You would!' he remarked, not sparing a glance to his elder sister. 'It grows cool now the breeze is up. You should take Father indoors.'

Hester compressed her lips as she moved to do Andrew's bidding, pausing as she passed Charlotte and inclining her head. 'I'm sorry if I spoke out of turn, Charlotte. It was not my place.'

'Of course it was! You are as a sister to me,' responded Charlotte clearly. 'I welcome and value your opinions, Hester.'

Wheeling the Captain's chair, Hester withdrew into the morning-room, closing the glass door behind her.

Charlotte at once spun around to confront Andrew, her eyes sparkling angrily. But even as she drew breath to speak, he caught her shoulders lightly, his manner and his tone quite altered.

'Lottie dear, if you proceed with this folly, you do so without my blessing and against my wishes,' he began softly. 'However, if you truly believe it is your best course, then so be it. I humbly apologise for my outburst.'

'Andrew,' she looked up into his face, her gaze held fast by his. 'I never want there to be cross words between us.'

'Then perhaps you shouldn't be so head-strong and stubborn!' He laughed as he kissed her. 'Although I would have you no other way! The weather seems set fair, shall we take a picnic out to the abbey ruins?'

'I'd like that very much! I have a few errands this morning, but they shouldn't take long.'

'Splendid!' Slipping his arm about her waist, he drew her close to his side as they strolled across the garden. 'I'll instruct Mrs Dawber to prepare a basket, have Will make ready the gig, and we'll set off upon your return from the village!'

Charlotte was hurrying through the village after spending an hour or so reading to Widow Tunstall, when she bumped into Bessie Proud coming out from the cobbler's.

'They've picked the new vicar, miss!'

Bessie exclaimed as the pair walked to-gether. 'A Lancashire man, he is. With a family of young bairns. Him and his missus came to the church and asked me if they could have a look around the parsonage. I didn't think you'd mind, so I let 'em in. They've asked me to stay on and keep house for them. Such a nice couple, they are. St Hild's is his first charge, so he was saying…'

Charlotte was glad Bessie was to keep her place at the parsonage.

Although she continued to visit several times each week, it deeply distressed her to go there now. All of the Vale's belongings were ready for removal to The Old White Bear on the day before the auction and the once cheery, homely rooms that Charlotte knew so well were sad and bare, reminding her all too keenly of happier times.

Such melancholy thoughts kept her com-pany after she parted from Bessie at the stile, and she and Snuffy continued upwards through the beech wood and across the gar-dens of Gaw Hill. She entered at the side door and was passing the kitchen when Liddie hailed her.

'Miss!' The maid hurried out into the passage, drying her hands on her apron. 'You've a visitor! Miss Burdon. The eldest one. Asking for you especially, she is. Something about helping you with your rounds. At least that's what she told Miss Hester.' Liddie sniffed sceptically. 'Come with her ma, she did. They turned up – unexpected, I might say – just when Miss Hester was settled into a day's mending.'

Charlotte frowned. She hadn't spoken or heard from Sophy Burdon since before Pa died.

'I wonder what she wants?'

Liddie shrugged. 'Her ma's chit-chatting with Miss Hester and the Master in the back-parlour. I put Miss in the morning-room and offered her tea – although she looked ready for summat a fair bit stronger, *if* you take my meaning!'

'Thank you, Liddie.'

Charlotte took a deep breath. She'd planned to go straight upstairs to arrange her hair and dress, in preparation for her picnic with Andrew.

'I'd best go in.'

Sophy was on her feet and approaching Charlotte with outstretched hands the instant the morning-room door opened.

'The most dreadful thing has happened – Mama has found out about Ralph!' she exclaimed. 'One of her friends from the

Charitable Ladies' League saw us in town together and the old biddy immediately rushed to Mama and spread her vile gossip!'

'It was inevitable you'd be discovered sooner or later,' said Charlotte sensibly. 'I've seen you and Ralph twice myself.'

'Twice?' she queried. 'Surely there was only one occasion? But, no matter – Charlotte, I am relying upon your discretion and your assistance. Without you, I am quite lost!'

'Perhaps now that your friendship with Ralph is in the open,' began Charlotte, 'this is the opportunity for you to confide your feelings to your mother.'

'Despite all I've told you of my dilemma, you still don't realise the gravity of the situation, do you?' cut in Sophy curtly. 'My father died without sons, Charlotte! I am heiress to Egleton and Mama has but one intention for me. That I make an early marriage to a man wealthy enough to restore the family estates!'

'It's natural your mother wishes you to make a secure match,' began Charlotte, not unkindly. 'However–'

'Tucked away in your cosy little parsonage, you know nothing of society and its ways!' interrupted Sophy. 'My mother will sell me off to the highest bidder!'

Charlotte was horrified. 'But how can *I* help you?'

'Ralph and I were to have met today. Mama is watching me like a hawk, so there is no hope of my slipping into town for a tryst. Ralph will believe I no longer wish to see him.'

'Surely he'll realise there must be good reason for you not keeping your arrangement?'

'How can he? He can never call at The Crescent to learn the truth! Mama will not allow me out unchaperoned now and she will be scrutinising every letter and note I receive. Also, today's meeting is of particular importance, for Ralph is expecting an answer from me – he has suggested we elope.'

'And will you?' whispered Charlotte, her eyes wide.

'How can I?' retorted Sophy. 'Imagine the scandal. The disgrace that would be brought upon my family. Mama would disown me. I would be shunned by society. And however would we live? Where would we live? Ralph has a very junior position at the bank. I couldn't possibly marry him.'

'Then you would have refused his proposal?'

'Well, yes ... but I *do* want to continue seeing him, Charlotte! I *love* him,' she responded earnestly. 'Won't you keep my rendezvous at the Viennese this afternoon? This letter explains all to him – you must deliver it safely into Ralph's own hands.'

'Very well,' replied Charlotte after a moment. 'I will meet Ralph at the coffee house.'

'And will you contrive a way to bring a message from him?' persisted Sophy. 'It would mean so very much, and Mama will never for a moment suspect you! My only hope of escaping the house today was upon the pretext of meeting you about parish visits. Even then, Mama insisted on accompanying me!'

'I will do everything you ask, for I know you have nobody else to turn to,' Charlotte answered. 'But, please do not expect me to become your regular messenger. After today, I want no further part in your deceptions.'

'I'll never ask you another favour for as long as I live!' cried Sophy, kissing Charlotte upon both cheeks before turning to the glass above the mantle and adjusting her bonnet. 'I shall be at home all day tomorrow. You can come to luncheon and await the opportunity to pass Ralph's note to me. I'd best join Mama and Hester now. Oh!'

She paused, her hand upon the morning-room door.

'I was sorry to hear about Reverend Vale. And your actually seeing the accident – I can't bear to even think of witnessing such a ghastly thing!'

Sophy swept from the room and, left alone, Charlotte sank on to the couch. She drew in a deep breath, her fingers loosely knotted in her lap.

'Well, there's a pretty pickle!' declared a man's voice, and she spun around to see Andrew emerging from the breakfast-room in the adjoining alcove, a folded newspaper in his hands.

'I heard every word, Charlotte, I'm sorry. I didn't intend to eavesdrop. I was reading in the alcove and didn't even realise anyone had come into this room until I heard you and she start talking,' he explained apologetically. 'It immediately became such an intimate conversation that I couldn't declare my presence and just barge in. It was altogether exceedingly embarrassing. And you, my dearest Lottie, are unwillingly enmeshed in this intrigue?'

'I wish it were not so!' she declared with

feeling. 'It began by chance when I saw Sophy with a young man in the Viennese coffee house.'

He shook his head when the whole tale was told.

'And do you believe this saga of desperate family fortunes and vulgar marriage settlements?'

'I'm afraid I do,' she answered simply. 'Sophy appears a highly-strung and passionate girl, and perhaps she does embellish her story, but I don't doubt the Burdons' circumstances are much as she describes them.'

'Sophy Burdon may have the face and voice of an angel – for to hear that young lady sing is to glimpse Paradise – however, I wager her nature is not the least angelic!'

'That's unfair! You can't fault her for not wanting to be forced into a loveless marriage!'

'From the little I know of Mrs Burdon, she certainly does exhibit all the signs of a fiercely ambitious mother – however, she is not the only member of that family with a mercenary streak,' he remarked dryly. 'Despite her daughter's protestations of love for this character Ralph, Sophy has no intention of marrying him because the poor blighter is not yet rich! I wouldn't waste a deal of sympathy upon your friend's predicament, Lottie!'

'Sophy Burdon isn't my friend,' returned Charlotte tersely. 'Nonetheless, I gave her my word I'd deliver her letter to Ralph Kirrige.'

'Then, as soon as Will brings around the gig, we'll set off for our abbey picnic and afterwards go down into the town to meet the lovestruck swain.'

'You're coming with me?'

'I'm not about to let you attend a furtive assignation with a total stranger, Lottie! This entire situation is sordid and quite improper. Sophy should not have presumed upon your kindness,' he said soberly. 'I'm concerned about your entanglement in such deception, and I'm asking your permission to take your place at The Crescent tomorrow. I shall advise Mrs Burdon that you're indisposed but have asked me to deliver a book – or music, perhaps – that you had promised to lend Sophy. On that pretext, I'll gain an opportunity to pass on any letter from Mr Kirrige. And that shall be an end to our involvement with the Burdon family's sorry affairs.'

'But Andrew, I promised I'd do it!'

'Providing all is done according to her

180

instructions, do you imagine Sophy will give a fig who is messenger?' He grinned, kissing Charlotte's upturned face. 'Leave it to me, darling. I'll take care of everything. Now, off you go to change and then we'll be on our way to the abbey ruins!'

'Miss Vale!' Zachariah Mylecraine emerged from his office at the rear of the draper's, consulting the heavy gold pocket watch upon his waistcoat. 'You may now cover your counter. The warm weather is encouraging our customers to think about new dresses – your muslins have been busy today!'

'Very busy, sir,' replied Charlotte, carefully draping clean linen sheets across the bolts of fine fabrics stacked up along her counter. 'The lavender and azure spotted are especially popular, and we're running low on both.'

'Then, before you go home this evening, write up an order for further supplies. Our customers must never be disappointed!' The draper turned upon a well-polished heel and strode towards his office, casting a side-long glance to the mousy woman in charge of flannels. 'Miss Caruthers, a word please...'

Charlotte presently left the shop by the

side door. Raising her face to the warmth of the evening sunlight, she hurried through town to the coffee shop.

She and Madge Prentise kept in touch by meeting twice each month after work and treating themselves to pastries.

'Mmmm, damson puffs!' sighed Madge, savouring the feather-light confection and succulent fruits. 'Sheer luxury! So, have you heard from your ma and Lucy? How did the christening go? Did the poor little mite cry his eyes out? All my nephews did when they were baptised!'

'I got a letter just the other day,' replied Charlotte, cutting into her Parisian slice. 'The sun shone, and baby Jacob was as good as gold! Lucy said it was a perfectly beautiful day and Ma looked lovely in her bonnet!'

'That's wonderful. And how are things with you, Charlotte?'

'Well, Mr Mylecraine must be satisfied with my work, because he's starting to give me more responsibilities.'

'That's very good, but it's not really Zachariah Mylecraine that I'm interested in,' returned Madge bluntly. 'Tell me all about Master Andrew Holcomb! Eee, if only I'd seen him first and were twenty years younger, you'd not have stood a chance. Nor would he, come to that!'

Charlotte laughed. 'Actually, I see less and less of Andrew with each passing week! He's so busy with the Holcomb Line; he's always here in town.'

'Only to be expected, isn't it?' replied Madge sympathetically. 'The lad's bound to want to make a big success of it all – especially if he has *matrimony* on his mind!'

'I think I'll have another cup of coffee,' commented Charlotte blandly. 'How about you?'

'You've no need to go scratching round the woods for berries,' commented Will, straightening up from hedging as Charlotte passed by with her basket. 'Garden yonder's full of 'em!'

'I know!' She laughed, bundling Snuffy over the stile into the wood ahead of her. 'But I like gathering wild fruit – it's somehow very satisfying.'

'Aye, it is that.' He hesitated, adding. 'Give me a minute and I'll fetch a trug!'

The dappled shade of the old wood was welcome after the sun's brilliance. Cool softness enveloped them as they strolled beneath the leafy canopy seeking out bundles of tiny, sharp raspberries entangled amongst thorny hawthorn, gorse and thistle.

'Will, I've never properly thanked you for carrying our belongings from the parsonage to the Old White Bear. Or for being there for the auction,' she said quietly as they walked. 'I'd intended going myself but when the day came, I just couldn't face seeing all our things sold off like that.'

'Ah, it were nowt,' he responded, smiling down at her. 'I shall always treasure your pa's books, Charlotte. I know how precious they were to him.'

'He'd be so happy at your giving a good home to his little library!'

They were nearing Charlotte's old home now. Children were laughing and playing in the garden and there was washing drying on the green.

Snuffy ran on ahead, scratching excitedly at the worn gate until Charlotte called her back. 'I can't seem to get used to other folk being at the parsonage. I somehow still half expect to see…'

'It'll take a lot more time than it's been, lass,' chipped in Will gently. 'You're all right at Gaw Hill though, aren't you? You and Hester seem really close, and Master thinks the world of you – Snuffs, too!'

'The Captain's such a kind man, and Snuffy's devoted to him. Instead of coming for a walk with me, I think she would have happily stayed at his side today!'

'Dogs sense things we don't.' Will bent to ruffle the collie's woolly coat. 'She knows he's not too good these days.'

There was something in his voice that startled Charlotte, and she looked at him sharply.

'No. It's nowt anybody's told me, lass. It's just... I've known and loved that old man my whole life. He took me in, gave me a name and a home and now ... now I feel I'm near to losing him.'

'Oh, Will!' Her own loss was still so very raw, and tears sprang immediately to her eyes as she instinctively wrapped her arms about him, holding him tight and close and comforting him as she might a child. 'It might not be so...'

'Dr Hawkes seems satisfied enough with him, but Master's growing frailer by the day. I can see it in his eyes.'

'I'm so very sorry!'

'Nature's taking her course, I reckon.' He looked away, fixing his attention upon a thread of primrose wool clinging to her skirts. 'What is it you're knitting?'

'A fine summer shawl for Ma's birthday,' she answered, keeping her voice light. 'It's crocheted, actually. A really pretty shell pattern to remind her of the sea!'

'I'd not thought, but Tarnwithe's land-locked, isn't it?' he remarked. 'I'd not care for that; being hemmed in by mountains and great tall hills. I'd miss being able to stand on the shore and look at nowt but sky and ocean!'

They emerged from the shadowy greens of the wood on to the cliff path. Despite the shimmering heat above the ebbing tide, there was still a whisper of fresh salt breeze.

Charlotte took in a deep breath. 'I'd miss this if I went away.'

'Aye, me too,' he murmured, standing at her side and following her gaze far across the hazy beach. He could smell the fragrant rosemary infusion she used to rinse her hair and glancing down at her, saw the silky curls clinging damply to the nape of her neck. He cleared his throat. 'So, you're crocheting a shawl for your ma's birthday. That'll be nice.'

'I always make a marchpane cake for her at Christmas time and for her birthday, too,' she went on, still gazing far away. 'I'll leave the baking until nearer the time, though. It's not a cake that improves with keeping.'

'I used to look forward to your sultana scones with a big mug of Bessie's tea.' He grinned. 'I miss your baking!'

'I miss doing it,' she admitted, as they turned their backs on the shore and entered the coolness of the wood once more. 'I don't cook at all any more. Mrs Dawber runs her kitchen at Gaw Hill like clockwork and I'm certain she wouldn't welcome intruders!'

'She's fierce, but she makes a decent enough rice pud!' He paused, adding seriously, 'You *are* settled and happy at Gaw Hill?'

'More so than I ever could have hoped for,' she answered. 'What of you, Will? You and Andrew? It pains me to watch you so often at odds.'

He shrugged. 'We don't have much to say to each other these days.'

'It's such a shame. We were all once so close!'

'Charlotte, I'm not sure how to say this – and you'll hate me for it anyhow – but say it I must,' he began awkwardly, touching her arm so that she stopped walking and faced him. 'Andrew doesn't confide in me. Nor have I seen or heard anything. It's just a hunch, sort of. But I – I believe Andrew might be seeing somebody else – a girl, that is. I just don't want you to get hurt because I didn't speak out,' he finished hurriedly. 'I hope I'm wrong.'

'I'm certain you are mistaken,' Charlotte said softly, touching a gentle hand to his cheek. 'Dear Will – I could never hate you! I know well you are only concerned for me, but Andrew would never hurt or deceive me. Come along, we've gathered enough berries.' She slipped her arm through his as in their carefree youthful days. 'Let's return to Gaw Hill and I'll brave the wrath of Mrs Dawber to bake some raspberry buns!'

The week before her mother's birthday, Charlotte was in Hild Head village with Hester buying ingredients for the march-pane cake.

'I've got the other things, but I didn't buy any almonds,' she told Hester when she came out from the grocer's. 'They looked too dry and hard. I don't think they'd grind well.'

'Probably old. I don't suppose Mr Ent-wistle sells many almonds. You'll get fresher in town.'

'I suppose so. I was hoping to bake the cake this evening, if that's all right.'

'Whenever you choose, Charlotte. You must always make use of the kitchen as you wish,' replied Hester as they walked. 'There are one or two things I might get in town myself. Why don't we go home and fetch the gig? We'll have to drive ourselves because Will and Father are playing chess, but we could do our shopping, have luncheon somewhere nice, then listen to the band playing in the Gardens and make a proper day of it! What do you say?'

They had a lovely morning in Whitby and, their purchases completed, the two women enjoyed a light and leisurely luncheon before strolling towards the Floral Gardens. Charlotte immediately recognised the Burdons' carriage waiting outside the fashionable Hotel Excelsior and saw Andrew and Mrs Burdon, deep in conversation, descending the hotel's marble steps together.

'I wonder what business Andrew has with Clara Burdon?' mused Hester, also noticing the couple. 'Let's hurry into the Gardens! If they see us, Mrs Burdon is certain to keep us late – that woman can talk the leg off a milking stool – and we don't want to miss the music starting!'

The marchpane cake was baked and sent

with the crotcheted summer shawl up to the Lakes in good time for Edith Vale's birthday.

On the day itself, Charlotte rose early and, with permission from the new vicar's wife, gathered an armful of fragrant summer blooms from Ma's flower garden at the parsonage. She went across into the church-yard, kneeled at the place where Pa rested and arranged the flowers just as Edith had asked her to.

It was as she was making her way back across the churchyard that she caught the murmur of voices from the west door of the church, just a few yards away, and she half-turned just as the new vicar was showing out a tall man who had a pretty, golden-haired woman on his arm. The young couple were well known to her.

Andrew started, but in the merest heart-beat regained his composure.

'Lottie! I had not planned to make an announcement yet, however...' he began smoothly, glancing towards the girl at his side. 'I have made Miss Burdon an offer and she has accepted. Sophy is to be my wife.'

Troubled Times

The newly-weds honeymooned in London and Bath before travelling north so that Andrew might visit his newly-acquired hall and estates at Egleton.

On the morning after the couple's return to Gaw Hill, he caught up with Charlotte in the cobbled stable yard as she made for the wood to walk Snuffy.

'I daresay you're accustomed to this ungodly hour, Lottie,' he commented, wincing at the dazzling brilliance of the autumnal sunrise. 'Myself, I think it positively uncivilised to be abroad so early! Needs must, however. I am to see the lawyers first thing and, of course, must go into the Holcomb Line offices to ensure all has been well during my absence.'

Tongue-tied, Charlotte quickened her pace, her head bowed. This was the first occasion they'd been alone since that day at St Hild's when Andrew had announced his engagement to Sophy Burdon. The sharp pain that had sliced through her then was all the keener now, for now she had to endure looking upon Andrew as a man married to another, and witness his tender looks and gestures of togetherness towards his bride.

His arm brushed hers as they walked. He was conversing carelessly, but she could not respond. Her voice would surely betray her, exposing the unbearable yearning deep within her for the man she had lost.

'The manor-house at Egleton is very old-fashioned and in need of great refurbishment before I'd consider it habitable,' Andrew continued, drawing on his gloves. 'Nonetheless, the structure is sound. I've had surveyors rigorously examining every stone, stick, field, farm, mill, workshop and tenant. The raw material is present in abundance at Egleton, it merely requires efficient management and overseeing. I've already installed my own man up there.

'While staying at the Duchesneys' plantation in Carolina, I saw how to make land and labour work for you,' he concluded, glancing around as Will led Caesar from his stable. 'Just a year ago I was sipping juleps and playing cards on a Mississippi riverboat, and now I am Squire of Egleton with a few thousand-odd acres, and I can't quite recall how many tenants. How swift fortune might change!'

'Came at a pretty price though, did it?' commented Will, handing the reins to Andrew. 'Your mount, sir.'

Andrew ignored the remark, swinging up into the saddle.

'Be sure to see the wheelwright today, Will. And take the bay mare to be shod. Mrs Holcomb wishes to ride each day, and the bay mare is our most docile beast.'

He glanced down at Charlotte, raising his hat to her and bestowing upon her a smile that drained her senses.

'Good morning to you, Lottie. Enjoy your walk!'

Caesar's hoofs clattered away over the cobbles as Andrew nudged him into a canter and Will uttered an oath under his breath, directing the epithet at his former friend's receding figure.

'What did he have to say for himself,' murmured Will, taking in Charlotte's pale countenance and the dark rings beneath eyes that had seen little rest. 'Apart from swaggering about acting like the lord of the manor and master of all he surveys?'

'Not much,' she replied quietly, stooping to fuss Snuffy who was impatient to be off.

'I can't look him in the face now without

itching to flatten him!' exclaimed Will. 'And if he carries on like this, I swear I'll not be able to stop myself!'

'That's not your way, Will,' she returned mildly, looking up at him with a sad smile. 'Never was, and never will be.'

'Happen not, but he has it coming, Charlotte. After what he did to you.'

'Andrew – Andrew is blameless in the matter,' she said, stumbling at the emotion of simply speaking his name. 'I assumed, because I had certain feelings, that he must share them. He never made any promises or declarations to me. Not a one.'

'Don't make excuses for him, Charlotte!'

She shook her head. She'd spent the past weeks wondering what might have been – *if* Andrew had not been in the alcove and overheard that conversation with Sophy. *If* he had not gone the next day to the Burdons' home at The Crescent with the letter from Ralph Kirrige and sought a moment alone with Sophy to deliver that message...

'If sheer chance had not caused their paths to cross as it did,' she murmured. 'Perhaps they would never have fallen in love.'

'Love?' exclaimed Will derisively. 'Surely you don't think love had anything to do with their match, Charlotte?'

She faltered. 'Perhaps it wasn't so for Sophy, but Andrew wouldn't wed somebody he didn't truly love. You can't choose not to love a person, Will, anymore than you can make love happen where it doesn't truly exist.'

'I know that well enough.' He paused, pushing a hand through his tousled hair. 'It's a grand morning, and the tide'll just about be up. Do you mind if I come with you to the beach? I'll just fetch my coat...'

He disappeared into the stables and Charlotte went around the corner to give Snuffy a drink at the pump. She heard Liddie's shout from the side door.

'Will! You're not off out are you? Mrs Holcomb says she wants the carriage waiting!'

'Wants it right this minute, does she? At the crack of dawn?'

'The missus just rang for her tea and said she wants the carriage waiting.' Liddie shrugged. 'Don't go biting my head off, Will Jervis!'

'Sorry, Liddie.' He exhaled. 'Aye, it'll be all ready, waiting and gleaming for whenever her ladyship pleases.'

'You can be a right sarky beggar, you can...' Liddie began, breaking off as she caught sight of Charlotte coming back around from the pump. 'Oh, there you are, miss! I've been looking for you all over the house! Mrs Holcomb says to tell you she wants you to help with her hair and her dresses after breakfast, so you're to go up to her room then.'

'Oh! Thank you, Liddie,' replied Charlotte, taken aback as the maid bobbed a curtsey and disappeared indoors.

'You're surely not–' Will stared in disbelief. 'She can order me about to her heart's content, but not you! You're a friend of the family. Do her hair and her frock indeed! Who does she think she is?'

'She's Andrew's wife.'

'Aye, but you're not her servant,' he returned hotly. 'Pah, some friend she's showing herself to be!'

'Sophy Burdon was never my friend, but nor is she my enemy.' Charlotte raised imploring eyes to his. 'I'm certain she had no inclination of my feelings for Andrew – why ever would she? It would be so easy and so very wrong of me to resent and dislike her simply because Andrew chose her and not me. But my unhappiness is not Sophy's fault.'

'I'd put nowt past that conniving little minx!' returned Will. 'With her fluttering eyelashes and winsome smile– I'd not trust her as far as I could throw her!'

'She finds herself part of a family she hardly knows. She's sure to be nervous and to need help settling in.'

'That'll be why she's dishing out orders left, right and centre,' agreed Will scathingly. 'But I can seen you're determined to give her the benefit of the doubt.'

Later that morning, Charlotte went upstairs in response to Sophy's summons. Standing on the gallery outside the bedchamber which had been freshly papered, draped and carpeted in readiness for the newly-weds occupancy, she faltered, drawing in a deep breath, her hand hovering a second or two before tapping softly upon the smooth oaken door.

'Ah, there you are! I'm visiting Mama and my sisters today.'

Sophy was finishing her breakfast, sitting propped against plump pillows with her hair falling loose about her shoulders in soft curls.

'I had several dresses made while we were in London and I asked that foolish girl to set them out for me, but she has not the slightest idea of how to wait upon a lady!'

'Liddie is far from foolish and she works very hard in the house, Sophy,' murmured

Charlotte uneasily.

Andrew's neckerchief lay thrown across the back of a chair and the very air bore traces of the fresh, clean smell of his shaving soap and pomade.

'I realise that Hester isn't the sort to have need of a lady's maid,' considered Sophy, sipping her coffee. 'However, I must have someone to attend me! I'm Andrew's wife. I must always ensure he is proud for me to be so!'

From where Charlotte was standing at the foot of the high, four-poster bed, she could see the impression upon the pillow next to Sophy's where Andrew's head had lain.

'The dresses are behind you in the wardrobe. We'll decide what I'm to wear later,' went on Sophy. Stretching her arms above her head, she slipped from the bed and padded barefoot to sit before her glass, inclining her head to left and then to right. 'Be a dear and prepare my bath, Charlotte. Oh, I do hope that hired man has the carriage waiting! He's so incredibly rude and surly. Between you and I, I am not at all impressed with the servants here. After I've bathed, you can dress my hair. Andrew prefers me to wear it so.' She swept up her ringlets between her fingers. 'Can you…?'

The discreet knock upon the door did not wait upon a response. The door swung open and Hester stood on the threshold.

'Good morning, Sophy. I hope you slept well?' she began pleasantly. 'I've asked Liddie to come up and help you dress.'

'Please! Not that awful girl! Charlotte will please me far more!'

'That's as maybe, however Charlotte is not a servant,' replied Hester firmly, her keen gaze taking in the fact that Charlotte was setting fresh towels to warm before the fire. 'If you wish to engage a lady's maid, I'm sure that can be arranged. Ah, here's Liddie! Charlotte and I will retire and leave you to your toilet.'

'I don't want there to be bad feelings between you and Sophy on my account,' said Charlotte as the two women started downstairs together.

'I'll not have you treated in such a fashion, Charlotte. The girl's arrogance is beyond belief! She's already kept Will dressed and waiting the whole morning to take her out in the carriage, when he could've been in the library reading to Father! You know how much Father enjoys that.

'Sophy may well be Andrew's wife, however, she is *not* mistress of Gaw Hill!' finished Hester softly, her clear gaze meeting Charlotte's. 'And I will not permit her to ride roughshod over members of my household!'

Charlotte's mood was bleak when she and Madge next met at the Viennese for their regular get together over coffee and pastries.

'I think about Andrew constantly,' confided Charlotte, her eyes downcast. 'It *hurts* to be near him and yet...'

Madge's forehead creased with concern for her friend. 'Won't he be moving to that place of his wife's that he's now Squire of?'

'Egleton? Perhaps, one day, I suppose,' considered Charlotte. 'Andrew said the manor-house isn't habitable yet and he's put someone in charge of the estates. Besides, he has to stay in Hild Head to run the Holcomb Line.'

'All I know of Sophy Burdon is what I saw of her in the shop, and she struck me as a right little madam,' remarked Madge.

'It's not really her fault, Madge. Sophy's been brought up differently from us. On the whole, everything goes along amicably enough.'

Charlotte stirred sugar into her coffee.

'It's the evenings at Gaw Hill that are most

difficult, you know; after supper, when we're all sitting together quietly in the drawing-room during the hours before going up to bed... Hester and I will usually be reading or stitching, and the Captain will be dozing while Sophy plays the piano and sings. She does both beautifully. Andrew can't take his eyes from her.'

'Perhaps you could go up to the Lakes and visit your ma and sister?' suggested Madge gently. 'At Christmas time, maybe.'

'I have thought about getting away,' answered Charlotte. 'Not just for a visit, but for good.'

'You're never thinking of leaving Gaw Hill!' exclaimed Madge, aghast. 'The Holcombs are like family to you.'

Charlotte raised anguished eyes, her voice barely a whisper.

'I'm not sure I can bear it much longer!'

'Don't you go losing your head and making a rash decision you'll likely regret for the rest of your life,' warned Madge fervently. 'I lost my husband to the war in the same year we wed. I've never had any inkling to marry another, but it's hard, Charlotte. Very hard. Without family, a woman has no place to belong. Nobody to belong to. Life gets a bit colder and lonelier with every year that passes. At Gaw Hill, you've a safe home and you've decent folk there who care about you – don't throw all that away on account of a man who's no good anyway.'

The crystal lamps cast a pool of warm, soft, golden light upon Sophy as she played and sang. The drawing-room's heavy curtains were closed against the chill autumn night and Captain Holcomb sat dozing at the fireside, soothed by the melody, while Charlotte and Hester sat together upon the couch with their needlework.

As she embroidered a linen runner, Charlotte was aware of Andrew's stillness as he sat in the winged chair, a glass of cognac warming in his cupped hands and his gaze distant, staring into the dancing firelight and listening to his wife making music.

'Delightful, Sophy!' He looked to her with a smile, watching her as she rose from the piano stool and came to his side, her finger-tips lightly brushing the nape of his neck.

'I'm pleased you enjoyed it.' Perching upon the arm of his chair, she dropped a light kiss on to his forehead before glancing across the fire towards the slumbering elderly man. 'It's one of the Captain's favourites.'

Hester followed her sister-in-law's gaze

fondly, her gaunt face softening into a smile.

'Father's always loved that piece, Sophy. It was one of Mother's favourites, too. And Andrew's right, you do play so very beautifully. I've always wished to be musical, but I don't have any talent whatsoever!'

'There are simple pieces not so difficult to play. Perhaps I could teach you,' replied Sophy. 'By the way, I've invited Mother and my sisters to luncheon on Thursday.'

'That'll be nice! It's high time they came to visit us,' responded Hester. 'Be sure to let Mrs Dawber know we're to have guests.'

'I already have. I told her yesterday, actually,' went on Sophy, adding, 'Andrew and I have been married some while, and I believe I should have the keys to the house now, Hester.'

Charlotte heard Hester's gasp, and glanced sidelong to see the colour leeching from the older woman's face.

'Gaw Hill's keys?' Hester's voice was barely audible. 'B-but—'

'Gaw Hill is Andrew's home and I am Andrew's wife, Hester,' continued Sophy smoothly, her hand resting upon his shoulder. 'I want the keys.'

Hester's agitated gaze went to her sleeping father, then turned sharply to her brother.

Andrew merely shrugged, and Charlotte was shocked at his lack of interest. This matter, which was of the greatest importance to Hester, was clearly of no consequence at all to him.

'Sophy's my wife. If it pleases her to have the keys, she must have them.'

'If you have any objections–' In a rustle of silk, Sophy moved as though to waken Captain Holcomb. '–perhaps your father might decide?'

'That won't be necessary.' Hester's reply was as swift as it was dignified. Picking up her work bag, she rose to leave the room. 'I shall fetch the keys.'

The instant the door closed behind her, Charlotte rounded upon the newly-weds, her hazel eyes blazing. 'How can you be so cruel? Is your selfishness such that you care nothing for her distress?'

'You speak out of turn, Charlotte,' replied Sophy, her hand upon Andrew's. 'You forget yourself, I think...'

But Charlotte was no longer listening. Already halfway across the hall, she was running towards the stairs and towards Hester's little sitting-room.

When she reached it, the door was ajar and she could see Hester seated on the edge of the narrow bed, her hands clasped in her lap and her head bowed.

Charlotte was at once at her side, wrapping her arms about the woman's trembling shoulders. 'I'm so sorry!'

When at last Hester raised her face to look at Charlotte, her eyes were red-rimmed and filled with unshed tears. 'It's not just a set of keys, you know. It's my place she's taken from me!' she whispered brokenly. 'Gaw Hill and the family are my whole life. Now I shall have no purpose to my existence. I've become a useless old maid, utterly dependant upon the grace and favour of my brother and his pretty young wife!'

'It's despicable,' murmured Charlotte, watching Hester's unsteady hand removing the household keys from the drawer of her writing table. 'And – and it just isn't right!'

Hester didn't reply. Crossing to the wash stand, she splashed cold water upon her face before turning again to Charlotte.

'I don't want to give Andrew and Sophy the satisfaction of knowing I've wept.'

A short while later Charlotte watched as, straight-backed and composed, Hester started slowly downstairs to relinquish the keys and her place within her father's house.

The weeks slipped away into winter and, being out of the house working at Myle- craine's for much of the time, Charlotte saw little of Sophy's management of Gaw Hill.

She was certain Hester had had a quiet word with Liddie, Mrs Dawber and the others, urging them to do all they could to accommodate the wishes of their new mis- tress and so ensured the continued smooth running of the household.

One evening, coming home from Myle- craine's, Charlotte let herself in at the side door and overhead Liddie talking to Mrs Dawber.

'I don't know how she's putting up with it – having the young missus queen it over her all the time!'

'Miss Hester hasn't got much choice, has she? She's like us,' commented the cook grimly, banging a batch of dough on to the board. 'Just got to get on with it. Got no other family or friends to take her in, has she? She has to live here, and be grateful for it. Then there's the Captain needing to be cared–'

Hearing Charlotte's boots upon the stone- flagged passage, the two broke off their conversation, and were looking towards the doorway as she came into the kitchen, rubbing her hands.

'You look perished! Come and get warm.' Mrs Dawber smiled. 'Pot's hot, and there's shortbread still warm from the oven.'

Charlotte sat thankfully before the glowing coals, toasting her stockinged toes.

Fortified by the tea and shortbread, she went from the kitchen into the hall, pausing to look in upon the snug back-parlour, where Captain Holcomb and Hester increasingly tended to spend their evenings.

'Will's not long brought her back from the beach,' said Hester, as Snuffy bounded from her side to welcome Charlotte. 'She's fed and settled for the night.'

'That was thoughtful of him – I really didn't feel like going out again tonight!'

'It'll freeze, I'm sure,' agreed Hester.

'Going to be a hard winter,' mumbled Captain Holcomb, cocooned in a merino hat and rug despite the heat from the parlour's bright fire. 'Ship's are frozen up already.'

'I was reading the newspaper to Father,' explained Hester, glancing to Charlotte. 'It reported several ships – not ours; we don't sail the Arctic routes – are ice-bound and will remain so until the spring thaw.'

'Sad news.' Captain Holcomb sighed, his tired eyes closed. 'Sad news.'

'How dreadful for the sailors' families! All those months of worrying and waiting for them.'

'Whaling's a treacherous trade. Thank heavens we've never been involved in it,' remarked Hester, glancing across to ensure her father was sleeping before continuing softly. 'I sincerely hope Andrew does not have plans to change that!'

'Might he?' asked Charlotte in dismay.

'I've heard – not from Andrew, mind – that he's had several meetings with Fred Kirby. Kirby runs a fleet of whalers out of Whitby.'

By and by, Charlotte went upstairs to get ready for supper.

Passing along the landing outside their suite of rooms, she heard the murmur of Andrew's and Sophy's voices and the familiar pang of regret seared through her.

Entering her own room, she closed the door and stood a moment in the darkness, her back flat against the oaken panels. How on earth could she go on like this? Would the ache of loving and losing him never ease?

Washed and changed, she was just tidying her hair before going downstairs, when there was a quiet tap upon her door. She called out to whoever was there to enter, expecting to see Liddie or Hester, and was surprised when Andrew's new wife wafted into the room in a cloud of fragrance.

'You're looking weary and worn of late, Charlotte,' she said, sitting away from the fire at the curtained window. 'The daily walk to and from Whitby, together with working long hours at the draper's, must be exhausting.'

'It's hard work. However I enjoy being at Mylecraine's,' returned Charlotte, trying to keep an edge of irritation from her voice. 'As for the distance, it is a fair step but I don't find it exhausting.'

Sophy beamed, reaching forward to clasp Charlotte's hands.

'I have a proposal for you! I've discussed it with Andrew and he is in complete agreement. You are to give up that menial position at Mylecraine's immediately!'

'Give it up?' echoed Charlotte in consternation. 'I can't do that!'

'Indeed you can. You shall be my companion, Charlotte! I really do need someone – Liddie's only fit for the kitchen and I did consider engaging someone new. However, hired girls are often of the lowest class and thoroughly disagreeable, whereas you will be perfect!'

'I … thank you,' Charlotte began. 'But I don't want to leave Mylecraine's.'

'You don't understand, Charlotte. The arrangement is made. I wrote to Mr Mylecraine enquiring upon fabrics for my winter wardrobe and requesting he release you from his employment. I received his reply today. This is your final week at the draper's.'

Charlotte stared at her, aghast. 'Mr Mylecraine hadn't said anything about this to me!'

'Ah, that would be because I begged his indulgence that I might give you the news myself by way of a surprise! Now, I really must go down – I promised Andrew I would sing for him before dinner.'

The road north up into the quarry village of Tarnwithe became snowbound at the beginning of December, so Charlotte's thoughts of travelling to the Lakes and spending Christmas with Ma, Lucy and her family had to be abandoned.

Then the New Year brought with it the anniversary of her father's death, and she was engulfed with poignant memories. Her only consolation was being able to speak of Pa with Hester and with Will, who shared her grief.

While she'd been working in Whitby, days might pass without Charlotte even seeing Will Jervis. At least now, although she still missed her job at Mylecraine's, the two old friends were more able to enjoy each other's company.

Charlotte had quickly adapted to the unfamiliar duties of companion and lady's maid. Sophy went out a great deal; shopping, visiting and suchlike, and on these occasions Charlotte accompanied her, and Will drove the carriage.

Sophy also had a passion for riding – frequently spending the best part of a whole day away when she didn't have other engagements to fulfil – and whenever she was gone from Gaw Hill, Charlotte and Will would fall into their old habit of walking Snuffy along the beach together.

Upon such a morning in early spring, when frost still lay thick and sparkling upon the gardens and hills, Charlotte had helped her mistress dress and prepare for a day's riding. As soon as Sophy had gone down to the stable yard, Charlotte returned to her room to finish a letter to Ma and Lucy before popping it into the postbag.

She was just melting the sealing wax when

Hester looked in at her doorway.

'I won't keep you but a minute, Charlotte. I just wondered if Andrew's mentioned anything to you about how business is faring with the Holcomb Line?' she began earnestly. 'Last evening, I received another message from Jenkins – the head clerk at the office – it was he who advised me Andrew was meeting with Mr Kirby the whaler. It now appears Andrew is in furtive discussions with yet another unscrupulous individual – a Portuguese called Cristiano Maias.'

'Andrew has said nothing to me of this, but I know of the Portuguese. I've seen Andrew with him in town,' answered Charlotte honestly. 'It was a long time ago and Andrew wouldn't tell me anything about the man or how he knew him. And now, well, Andrew talks little to me, Hester.'

Hester placed a comforting hand on Charlotte's arm. 'Are you terribly unhappy?'

Charlotte shook her head. 'Andrew ... he is no longer the Andrew I loved.'

'You said *"loved"*. If that sentiment is truly passed, then I'm greatly relieved. For my brother is not worthy of your regard,' she said. 'Now away with you. Will is waiting. Enjoy your walk!'

The rippled sand was hard and crusted with frost, and the soft waves that crept up the shore were edged with ice as they gently flowed back to the sea before gathering momentum and slowly surging forwards once more.

Charlotte and Will strolled towards Jonas Rock with Snuffy wandering on ahead yet never straying from their sight.

'What a glorious morning!' exclaimed Charlotte suddenly, thrusting her hands into her pockets and raising her face to the brilliant blue sky. 'It's a real glad-to-be-alive day!'

'It's a real glad-her-ladyship's-gone-out-for-the-day day, more like!' Will laughed, stooping to retrieve something fallen from Charlotte's pocket.

'Oh, no! It's my letter to Ma and Lucy!' She frowned, vexed. 'I meant to put it in the postbag on my way out!'

'No matter. Instead of going on to Jonas Rock, we'll get back on to the cliff, cut across country and put your letter in at The Old White Bear – we'll be in plenty of time to catch the mail coach,' said Will. 'We'll have an inland walk for a change, and go over the hills above Hild Head in a big circle back to Gaw Hill.'

After leaving the letter at The Bear, they left the village behind them and walked through the valley up towards the hills. Despite there being ice on the beck there was real heat in the pale sun.

'It's almost warm enough for a picnic! I'm really looking forward to spring and summer this year, Will.'

He took Charlotte's hand, steadying her progress across the stepping stones and led her up on to the mossy bank.

'You and Snuffs stay here – I'll be back in a minute!'

'Where are you–' she broke off, laughing as Will jumped the stepping stones in single strides and was soon away over on the opposite bank and sprinting towards the farmhouse they'd passed on the walk up.

True to his word, he returned in a flash – with fresh bread, a wedge of cheese and a can of fresh milk.

'We'll climb to the brow of the hill, get a grand view and have that picnic!'

And that's what they. did. Charlotte stretched out on the coarse grass, leaning back on her elbows and drinking in the miles and miles of fields, meadows, hills, farms, and woods patchworked far below them.

A sudden movement away over by the

plantations caught her eye.

'Someone must have taken that old woodcutter's cottage,' she remarked, nibbling her cheese. 'See, there's a horse tethered outside?'

'Where? Oh, I can see now.' Will shifted his position for a better look. 'There are two horses. A roan and a bay!'

A quick glance passed between himself and Charlotte.

Then he shook his head, shielding his eyes against the sun to gain a clearer sight. 'It does look like the Holcombs' bay mare but, nay, you can't tell for sure from this – *Get down!*'

Grabbing hold of her shoulders, he pulled Charlotte face down alongside him on the grassy hillside.

'Best we're not seen, lass!' he hissed, keeping low to the ground as they watched a couple emerging from the woodcutter's cottage.

Charlotte couldn't stifle her gasp of amazement as she watched Sophy adjust her hat, then raise her face to kiss the man at her side.

'That's Ralph Kirrige!'

'Who? Is he the lad all them shenanigans were about before she wed Andrew?'

Will drew Charlotte sideways, out of the

couple's angle of vision, lest they glance around to the hill. 'Keep out of sight. It'll do us no good if it's known we've seen 'em.'

'Sophy and Ralph must be...' Her whisper faded to embarrassed silence.

'Aye, they must,' replied Will grimly. 'It seems Sophy and Andrew are better matched than I reckoned. Each is as faithless as the other!'

The brilliance of the rising full moon spilled silvery light into her room and disturbed Charlotte who, after a few sleepy moments, was wide awake. Turning on to her side, she plumped her pillow to gaze out at the starry sky. The hour was late and Gaw Hill was silent and in darkness.

She slipped from her bed, put on her dressinggown and padded downstairs to make a drink. In the kitchen, a single candle was burning on the kitchen dresser and Hester sat alone at the table, a cup of cold tea at her elbow.

'Couldn't you sleep, either?' Charlotte smiled at her.

'Haven't been to bed yet.' Hester sighed wearily. 'I'm waiting for Andrew to come home. I've had another note from Jenkins. That man is not given to stirring trouble,

216

and if he suspects Andrew is involved with underhand business, then I believe him! Andrew may not owe *me* any explanations of his actions, but if even half of what Jenkins suspects is accurate, then Andrew certainly owes Father the truth of his intentions!' concluded Hester hotly. 'I'm determined to have this out with him.'

Charlotte put some milk to heat and sat down opposite Hester with a sigh. 'Perhaps Andrew's working late?'

'Perhaps he isn't!' declared the older woman in exasperation. 'Why can't he be happy with what he has, Charlotte? He stays out late too many nights. He'll be at the Black Jack Tavern most likely. Drinking, gambling, womanising, squandering this family's hard-earned money. And all the while neglecting the very business that puts the money into his pocket!'

Charlotte rose, mixing cocoa powder and sugar in their cups before pouring on hot milk, and offering the drink to Hester.

'You look exhausted. Why don't you take this and go up to bed?' she suggested kindly. 'Get some sleep? Even if Andrew does come in now, he'll probably be in a foul mood.'

'I'll tackle him in the morning, when he's sober and I'm thinking straight!' agreed

Hester, taking the hot cocoa.

Charlotte took her own drink to her own room and read until her eyelids grew heavy, then she blew out her light and turned on to her side.

The next thing she knew, Will was at her bedside shaking her awake.

'Shh, it's only me!'

She sat bolt upright. 'Is it the Captain...?'

'Nay, nay. Nowt like that, thank the Lord,' he reassured her hurriedly, his voice low. 'It's Andrew. He's been drinking and carousing at a tavern in the town and is plenty the worse for wear. I've got him in the stables. Can you come down and give me a hand...?'

Touching a flame to the stable lantern, Will hung the light from one of the low beams and Charlotte saw Andrew sprawled across the hay, quite senseless. His clothing was torn and dirty and there was a cut on his head. A bubble of dried blood stained the corner of his mouth and the swelling around his eye and jaw was already darkening into bruises.

Charlotte at once dropped to her knees at his side.

'Will he be all right?'

'Aye. Whatever happened, I daresay he had

it coming.'

'Andrew's been fighting?' she gasped, horrified.

'That cheap scent you can smell isn't from who he fought with, more like who he fought *over!*' remarked Will, leading Caesar into his stall and removing his saddle and harness.

'I were asleep, and this lad from the tavern knocked me up and said I was to get into town as fast as I could and bring Andrew home. I had to lay him in the wagon and lead Caesar.'

'He looks dreadful. Is he badly hurt?'

'Broken ribs, I reckon, and that cut's pretty deep. He'd been drinking, of course, but the folk at the tavern said that it was during the fight that he just keeled over and passed out cold, so he's maybe taken some bad blows to his head.'

Will glanced over his shoulder at her as he rubbed down the wagon pony's rough, muddied coat.

'Hester has enough on her plate just now. I don't want her worried with this. Nor Master fretting over his son and heir, either. That's why I need your help. I cannot do it on my own.'

'I'll do anything that's needed,' she insisted, her gaze upon Andrew's face, but her hands tightly folded into her lap. 'Shouldn't we fetch Dr Hawkes?'

'Least fuss the better. Andrew can send for him tomorrow if he wants.'

Will was hurriedly feeding both horses as he talked, bedding them down for what remained of the night.

'We need to strap his chest and get him cleaned up. He'll need fresh clothes, too. Can you get them?'

She nodded. Since waiting upon Sophy, she'd become accustomed to the couple's accommodation and knew that all of Andrew's clothing was kept in the corner room he used for dressing.

'There's a divan in his dressing-room too. Sophy once told me that Andrew spends the night there when he's late back from Whitby and doesn't wish to disturb her.'

'Perfect! We'll have to get him upstairs and into that bed to sleep it off without waking the whole household!'

While they were putting Andrew to bed in the dressing-room, he briefly came round; his eyes unfocussed and straining to make out the shadowy figures before him.

'You fell off your horse,' murmured Will. 'We brought you home and put you to bed.

Go to sleep.'

However, Andrew's eyes were already closed and he'd drifted back into oblivion. It wasn't until they were safely in the kitchen again that Will and Charlotte were able to breathe a sigh of relief.

'Tea?'

'I'd not say no!' Will sat at the table, resting his head in his hands. 'By, they reckon history repeats itself, don't they?'

Charlotte eyed him curiously, putting the kettle to boil before sitting down beside him. 'Andrew was at the Black Jack Tavern tonight, wasn't he? And the owner is a Portuguese named Cristiano Maias?'

Will turned sharply to face her. 'What do you know of the Black Jack and Maias?'

Charlotte briefly related the occasions she'd seen Andrew with the Portuguese, concluding, 'Madge Prentise says the Black Jack's a den of vice. Is it?'

'Yes. But in its way, the Black Jack is also very … discreet. It's where wealthy gentlemen about town go to relax, have a few drinks, play cards and are entertained by the singers and dancers.' He grinned wryly. 'A den of vice, eh? Aye, I'd say your friend Madge has it about right!'

'Tonight Andrew was fighting over a girl,'

ventured Charlotte slowly. 'Has that happened before? Is that why he left Hild Head so unexpectedly all those years ago? It's time I knew, Will!'

He exhaled, leaning back in his chair to consider Charlotte's grave face.

'Andrew was always reckless and irresponsible – you were too young to see it – and when he got home from university that summer, he was out on the town practically every night. Happen Master thought he was just letting off steam before knuckling down to working for the Holcomb Line. But Andrew was wild. 'Course, a rich young gent like him with more money than sense was just the sort of regular customer Maias wanted in his tavern – easy pickings!'

'What exactly happened?' she persisted fearfully, Madge's sombre words still loud in her mind. 'Did – did Andrew have anything to do with that poor girl who died?'

'All I know is that he was at the Black Jack at the time. He'd been drinking, and him and this girl – only a young lass, she was – well, they were together in one of the rooms. The next morning she was dead. Andrew swore to his father and Hester that it was an accident. Said she'd tried to rob him while he was sleeping. He woke up, caught her going through his pockets. They struggled, and she fell and hit her head.'

Charlotte buried her face in her hands. So now she knew! However, Will was not yet finished.

'Thing was, folk who saw the girl's body said there were bruises around her neck.'

Charlotte could not contain a shocked cry.

'The way things are at the Black Jack, there would've been no fuss about the girl dying at all,' continued Will quietly. 'But it came out she was the daughter of a wealthy family from along the coast. She'd fallen out with her parents and run away from home!'

'It's horrible … but it *must've* been an accident!'

'The Captain paid Cristiano Maias to pull strings with his magistrate friends, to hush everything up and keep Andrew's name out of it,' concluded Will, draining his tea. 'Then he arranged for an old friend in Carolina to take Andrew into his home and Hester got him passage aboard the first ship sailing for the Americas.'

'Despite everything, despite the appalling way Andrew treats you now,' murmured Charlotte at length, 'you're still protecting him, aren't you?'

'Nay! Andrew should've been man enough

to face up to whatever happened in the Black Jack all those years ago,' retorted Will bitterly, scraping back his chair and rising from the table. 'Whatever I did tonight, I did it to spare the feelings of Hester and the Master. I'd not lift a finger to help Andrew Holcomb!'

'It's a pretty pass when a man's wife is so unconcerned for his health,' remarked Andrew, wincing slightly as Charlotte adjusted his pillows. 'And goes off riding without a care in the world!' he continued.

Charlotte said nothing, wondering if Sophy had gone to keep another assignation with Ralph Kirrige.

Andrew grinned crookedly at her, his face swollen and inflamed.

'Bring me the brandy bottle, Lottie – for the pain, you know.'

'Perhaps we should send for Dr Hawkes?'

'That old woman! No fear!' He sank back into the pillows, watching her moving about his room. 'You could fetch me something from the apothecary.'

'You really should see a doctor,' she persisted, worried by the severity of the bruising to his lower back and abdomen that she'd observed while helping Will strap his broken ribs.

Andrew took hold of her hand as she set down the decanter of brandy beside the bed. 'You and I are part of a conspiracy, Lottie. You know the truth of last night, but you will help me conceal it!'

'Why would I do that?' she retorted unsteadily, trying to free her hand but feeling Andrew's grasp tighten.

'You know why...' Taking her hand to his lips, he kissed each of her fingertips, all the while closely observing the flurry of emotions colouring her face. 'We *both* know why!'

Dragging herself free, she stepped out of his reach and moved towards the door. 'You're mistaken about my sentiments, Andrew! I will remain silent about the cause of your injuries, but only to spare your father and Hester distress. I'll fetch some medicine from the apothecary directly.'

'Am I never to have the opportunity of confronting my brother and demanding he explain his actions?' fumed Hester, tying her bonnet with a double knot.

She and Charlotte were in the hall preparing to walk into the village together.

'Fallen off his horse, indeed! If Andrew didn't drink so freely, he'd be less likely to fall off!'

'You've seen him this morning?'

'Oh, yes, I saw him! Playing for sympathy and lording it over everyone. Good practice, I suppose, for when he takes up his seat as Squire of Egleton!'

Hester fell quiet as they left Gaw Hill, her indignation seeming to unexpectedly ebb, leaving in its wake frustrated resignation.

'He'll never tell me what he's up to, Charlotte. Andrew will continue to taunt me and have sport at my expense for however long it amuses him.'

The two women duly completed their errands in Hild Head, with Charlotte acquainting the apothecary with Andrew's painful condition and purchasing several bottles of medicine and a box of powders.

When she and Hester returned to Gaw Hill late that afternoon, it was to meet Mr Jenkins just leaving the house.

'He must have seen Father!' cried Hester, picking up her skirts and rushing forward to speak with the company clerk. 'Jenkins! What brings you...'

Charlotte tactfully slipped past them and hastened indoors, only to hear raised, angry voices from behind the closed doors of the back-parlour.

Hester hurried into the house after her, crying out as she too heard the violent argument between father and son.

'No!' she shouted, running down the hall toward the parlour. 'Andrew must not–'

Even as Hester was about to burst into the room, the door was wrenched open and her brother stormed out.

'The Holcomb Line's *mine* now, Father! I shall do as I please with it!' he retorted bitterly. 'You and Jenkins can like it or go to the devil! It's nothing to do with either of you any more!'

Roughly pushing Hester aside, he strode down the hall, doubled-up slightly with one arm held tightly across his chest. Barging past Charlotte, he slammed from the house.

'Father, what's happened–?'

The old man shook his head, his face pale as parchment. Samuel Holcomb's faded blue eyes met Charlotte's as she hovered in the doorway.

'Fetch Will for me, lass.'

He looked up to Hester, standing beside his chair, her arm protectively about his shoulders.

'I'm for my bed. I'm tired, Hester – I'm dog-tired.'

Next day, Charlotte rose in good time to

give Snuffy a walk before beginning her duties for Sophy.

Treading noiselessly along the carpeted gallery, she saw Captain Holcomb's door wide open. Hester was seated in the bedside chair, her head bowed as she softly wept. She raised her face at Charlotte's gentle voice and consoling touch.

'He's gone,' she whispered. 'I came in with his tea as usual ... and ... Father's dead, Charlotte. And it is Andrew's fault!'

Charlotte looked in at Hester's sitting-room on her way out. These days, Hester was usually to be found tucked away up there in the room above the gardens. She no longer sat in the sunny back-parlour downstairs and, indeed, during the weeks since Samuel Holcomb's funeral, had rarely set foot in that once favourite room.

'Hester, I'm off to see Madge. Do you want anything from town? Better still, why don't you come with me? You'd enjoy meeting Madge and it's pleasant weather for the walk into Whitby.'

'Thank you, but not today.' Hester smiled, looking up from sewing a child's calico pinafore. 'I'm going to St Hild's later and want to finish this so I might put it into the parish poor basket. There are one or two other things, that I need to do in the village, also.'

Hester lowered her voice, mindful of the open door.

'I have an appointment with Father's solicitor. I want to ask Arthur if he can do anything to help Jenkins. I worry how he and his wife are managing.'

'Mr Jenkins isn't a young man, and without references...' agreed Charlotte. 'It won't be easy for him to find another position.'

'It will be impossible unless Arthur Glennister dispels the cloud my brother has cast upon his trustworthiness!' went on Hester. 'Father and Arthur Glennister were old friends, and he well knows the years of honest, exemplary service Jenkins has given the Holcomb Line. The poor man risked his livelihood by confiding to father and I his suspicions of Andrew's underhand dealings with the likes of Kirby and Maias,' she concluded. 'It would be dreadful if he was ruined because of his loyalty to our family and the Holcomb Line.'

Charlotte frowned, staring beyond Hester, out of the window across the gardens of Gaw Hill and beyond, to the green woods.

'Why is Andrew so often cruel and malicious these days, Hester? Why does he do it?'

'Because he can. And I have no power to stop him.' She paused, continuing in a brighter tone. 'Give my regards to your friend – I *would* very much like to meet Madge. Perhaps when I'm settled, we might all have supper together. I'd really enjoy that.'

Charlotte hurried downstairs, hoping to quit the house without confronting Andrew, but she was thwarted in this aim when he emerged from the library and blocked her progress along the hall.

'Ah, Lottie! How delightful you look – so flushed and pretty!' He grinned, tracing a finger along her cheekbone. 'I hardly see you of late. Are you avoiding me, by any chance?'

'Why would I do that?' she retorted curtly.

'Why indeed?' he mused, inhaling sharply as a sudden spasm of pain shot through his body.

'Drat!' he mumbled, as the pain subsided. 'That blighter at the Black Jack must've got in some lucky blows – I can still feel 'em! You'd best fetch more of those filthy medicines from the apothecary. They may taste vile, but at least they dull what ails me!'

'I'll collect them on my way home from Whitby.' She couldn't help but be concerned at Andrew's dark-ringed eyes and the pallor beneath the stubble of his unshaven beard.

'You'll have sufficient medicine until then? And you *will* send for Dr Hawkes if it gets worse?'

He nodded, one hand pressed to his lower chest.

'Make the most of your afternoon at the Viennese with the odious Madge Prentise, for there won't be many more.'

'Why won't there?' she demanded.

'Because I'm taking you up to Egleton.' He paused, reaching out to curl one of her ringlets about his finger, before tucking it into place at her neck. 'The manor-house will be ready by mid-summer. You'll like it there, Lottie. We're going to have some wonderful times together.'

'He never did!' exclaimed Madge, open-mouthed with astonishment as Charlotte brought her up to date with what had happened at Gaw Hill since they'd last met. 'I'd never have taken your Andrew for being such a bad 'un!'

'He's not *my* Andrew, and never was,' returned Charlotte shortly. 'He's ill and frequently in pain, but that does not excuse the appalling way he treats Will. And he's broken Hester's spirit completely.'

'Hardly surprising. What with him plan-

231

ning to sell out to a villain like Maias; Mr
Jenkins finding out and telling the Captain;
then Andrew going at it hammer and tongs
with his father about it all... Just too much
for the old man to bear, wasn't it?' reflected
Madge. 'Killed him. And then to sell Gaw
Hill out from under Hester – to *Cristiano
Maias* of all people!' She sucked air through
her teeth. 'I mean, it's Hester's home, isn't
it?'

Charlotte stared morosely into her un-
touched coffee. In her mind's eye, she was
seeing again that ghastly day after Samuel
Holcomb's funeral when Andrew had called
everyone, family and servants alike, into the
library at Gaw Hill and made his announcement. The Holcomb Line was all but sold to
Maias and now that Captain Holcomb was
dead and buried, Gaw Hill would also be
sold to the Portuguese businessman.

Hester had cried out that Andrew could
not do such a thing! Gaw Hill was her
father's house and her home! Andrew had
merely shrugged, and taken his time over
lighting another cigar.

'This is *my* house now, Hester; *my* home –
and I'm disposing of it. Never fear,' he went
on easily, 'you shall be provided for with an
adequate allowance to enable you to secure

suitable accommodation wherever you choose. In due course, Sophy and I will remove to my estate at Egleton and Charlotte will accompany us as my wife's companion. Meanwhile, Will Jervis and the rest of the servants have ample time to seek employment elsewhere.'

He drew upon the fine cigar, then exhaled the fragrant smoke and surveyed the horrified faces of the circle of people standing before him.

'Now, you may all go back about your business...'

It was Charlotte and Hester's day for cleaning at St Hild's, and after the constant tension pervading Gaw Hill, both welcomed the peace and tranquillity of the ancient church.

'I'll always be grateful to Arthur Glennister for clearing Jenkins' reputation and securing a suitable post for him with the Baltic Star company.'

'You did well for him, Hester.'

'All I did was speak to Arthur,' she replied, straightening stiffly from polishing the steps of the pulpit. 'He did the rest.'

'Have you given any thought to what you'll do?' began Charlotte awkwardly. 'For when...'

'When my brother signs our family home over to a villain?' Hester finished evenly. 'I've thought of little else. The notion that all Father and Mother worked so hard for, and everything that meant so much to them... It plagues me constantly, Charlotte. My mind has no rest. It's almost unbearable sometimes.'

Charlotte put a comforting hand upon the older woman's shoulder.

'Will you stay in Hild Head? Take a cottage here, I mean. Or in Whitby, perhaps?'

Hester shook her head. 'Knowing Maias will soon own my father's shipping company is bad enough, but I won't see that wicked man calling Gaw Hill his own! Better I go far away. I've a girlhood friend living in Harrogate. We haven't seen each other since she married and moved from Hild Head, but we've corresponded over the years. Dorothy's widowed now. We might take rooms together,' finished Hester, trimming the altar candles. 'What about you? Will you go to Egleton with them?'

'I don't yet know where I'll go, Hester,' replied Charlotte, packing up her basket of cleaning materials. 'But it certainly will not be to Egleton manor-house with Andrew and Sophy!'

Leaving Hester at St Hild's, Charlotte walked across country into the village to buy ink and a quarter of cinder taffy before returning to Gaw Hill.

Passing the stables, she saw no sign of Will. The wagon pony turned around in his stall at her approach, his ears twitching, and she went all the way inside to stroke his broad nose, then reached over the wooden partition to pat Caesar's sleek, glossy neck.

The bay mare wasn't in her stall. Sophy must still be out riding. Or pursuing her romance with Ralph Kirrige, if the pair were still seeing each other.

Leaving the cinder taffy where Will would find it, Charlotte went indoors.

Fetching a glass of cool lemonade, she wandered into the sun-filled morning-room. Although still early in the summer, the day was hot and the glass doors to the garden were flung wide open.

Gathering some cushions, she arranged them on the terrace and with her feet tucked beneath her, settled in the hazy sunshine to her reading.

A long shadow falling across her page was the first indication of Andrew's presence. She glanced up. He looked poorly. The broken ribs were all but healed; however his health did not improve.

Although he'd long since consulted Dr Hawkes, who was prescribing various treatments, the gradual deterioration in his condition continued. He'd lost considerable weight these past months and there was now a perpetual haggard greyness about his features, yet his eyes still burned with undiminished arrogance.

'How long is my sentence, Lottie?' he enquired curtly. 'How long do you intend to keep me waiting?'

'Sentence? Waiting?' she echoed, not even attempting to keep the irritation from her voice. 'Waiting for what?'

'You!'

He bent, gripping her shoulders and hauling her to her feet, knocking aside the book and lemonade so that the glass smashed upon the stone and scattered in glittering shards across the terrace.

'Something inside you is feeling *exactly* as I do, Lottie. You may deny that to yourself, but you cannot hide it from me!'

'Have you completely taken leave of your senses?' she demanded, pushing him away but unable to break free of his grasp. 'I did love you once, but I don't love you now. I *couldn't* love you now – not the man you've become! I don't even like you any more,' she continued, struggling vainly to extricate herself from his enveloping arms. 'Don't be ridiculous! You have a wife, remember!'

'Ah, the virtuous Sophy! Land marrying money! We've both got what we wanted, so far as it goes,' he murmured, taking a step forward and thus pressing Charlotte back against the sun-warmed stones of the wall. 'However, being wed to someone goes much further than that, you know ... and regarding those other aspects of marriage, I find myself wedded to completely the wrong woman. I want you, Lottie. Always have, actually.'

'Oh, for heaven's sake–' Flattening both palms against his chest and forcing him from her, Charlotte spun away towards the steps, but Andrew caught her arm, throwing her off balance and deftly pushed her down to the ground, using his weight to pin her there as his mouth hungrily sought hers.

'Andrew!' she gasped, averting her face. 'You're hurting–'

'Get off her!'

Charlotte squirmed around to see Will towering over them, the summer sky brilliant blue behind him.

Wrenching Andrew to his feet, Will drew

back a fist – then checked himself. Cursing under his breath, he shoved Andrew towards the open doorway.

'Be gone from my sight, man,' he muttered, kneeling at Charlotte's side and watching her attacker stagger across the terrace. 'You're nowt but a disgrace!'

'I'm all right, Will,' Charlotte murmured, red with embarrassment and shame as she scrambled upright, adjusting her dress. 'What you saw, it wasn't–'

'I know, lass, I know.'

He paused, gazing at her for another moment or two before slowly starting down the steps into the gardens.

'Get yourself a cup of hot sweet tea and steer clear of him. I'll only be in the stables if you want owt – oh, and thanks for the taffy!'

Shaken, Charlotte stood a while, inhaling deep, steadying breaths of the garden's fragrant air.

Andrew's strength had frightened her.

At length, she tentatively entered the morning-room – half-expecting him to still be lurking there. He was not. The room was empty.

She ran lightly through and across the hall, and her foot was already on the first stair before she caught sight of him, and gasped.

Through the open library door, she saw that Andrew Holcomb was lying face down and lifeless upon the Indian carpet.

The following days settled into a routine punctuated by Dr Hawkes' visits, and Sophy kept vigil by her husband's bedside as Andrew drifted in and out of a fitful, feverish stupor.

During lucid spells, he complained of pain and cramps.

When Sophy insisted a nurse should be engaged, he ordered his wife to hold her tongue and declared only Lottie should attend him.

Charlotte followed Dr Hawkes' instructions diligently. However, none of his prescribed medicines or treatments eased Andrew's growing discomfort.

He became weaker, with his fevers and lapses from consciousness becoming more frequent.

A Dreadful Accusation

'But you must go to Harrogate!' Charlotte insisted, the night before Hester was due to set off. 'In a couple of months, Gaw Hill will be sold and you need to find somewhere else to live! You and Dorothy have much to discuss and decide.'

'I don't like leaving you here, Charlotte. It isn't fair. Andrew isn't your responsibility.'

'Nor yours,' Charlotte continued gently. 'Don't worry so, Hester! Dr Hawkes comes in morning and night, and I have Will and Liddie. We'll manage fine. Besides, you and your old friend have had this trip planned for ages, and you can't let her down now!'

It was six days later, shortly after Dr Hawkes had completed his evening visit, that Andrew took a turn for the worse. Will had been sent to fetch Hawkes back, but there had been nothing the physician could do.

Andrew Holcomb had breathed his last and died just as Hawkes had been climbing the stairs to his sickroom.

'Charlotte, would you attend Mrs Holcomb?' the doctor suggested as he led Sophy away from Andrew's bedside. 'Perhaps you could–'

Sophy had been weeping inconsolably, her head bowed. But at Alan Hawkes' sombre words, she started violently.

'No, Doctor! No! Keep that woman from me!' she cried, her clear voice rising as she recoiled from Charlotte. 'She loved Andrew but he scorned her and married me! She hates me! She hated him – and now she's taken her revenge – Charlotte Vale has murdered my husband!'

'Dr Hawkes, you must act! I insist you immediately summon the constable and the magistrate,' snapped Sophy, her eyes dry and her cheeks flushed. 'Liddie, lock Charlotte into her room until the authorities arrive to arrest her.'

'But, ma'am, I – I–' The young serving girl looked horrified.

'Liddie–'

'It's all right, Liddie,' mumbled Charlotte numbly, her shocked senses stunned by the accusation.

She walked past the tearful maid and along the gallery to her room. Going inside, she heard Sophy's orders from without and the key was duly removed from the inside.

The door closed, and the key was turned fast.

In the twilight gloom of her silent room, Charlotte sank upon the bed and only then did tears spill from her eyes. She'd had little affection for Andrew of late, but she wept for their old days together and for the dear friend he had once been to Will and herself.

She hadn't noticed that the cacophony of voices along the gallery had ceased and that quietness had descended.

Only the scraping of a key in the lock startled her from her sad reverie.

The door edged open soundlessly.

'Charlotte!' the candle that Will was holding cast a thin light across her face. 'Why are you sitting in the dark?'

'I hadn't noticed...' she faltered. 'Andrew ... Andrew... He's dead, Will!'

'I know, lass. I know. And Sophy swears you poisoned his food while you were nursing him. Liddie came and told me all about it and gave me a key so that I might get you out!'

'Get me out?' she repeated blankly.

'Charlotte, you have to pack a bag. Just necessities, mind.' He dropped to his knees before her, cupping her cold, damp face between both his hands. 'We haven't got much time. The fuss Sophy's kicking up, we could have the constable and the magistrate and the whole blasted militia galloping up here at any minute!'

'Sophy doesn't mean what she's saying.' Charlotte sighed wearily. 'She's grief-stricken, Will.'

'Or cunning,' he returned grimly, pulling her to her feet and pushing her towards the wardrobe. 'I reckon Sophy's accusing you before anyone can think to suspect her!'

'Suspect Sophy?' She turned, bewildered, the open valise in her hands. 'Why would she want to harm Andrew?'

'Think about it! She married Andrew for his money. She's having an affair with Ralph Kirrige. Sophy's an adulteress who's likely going to be a very rich widow! How would *that* look to a judge and jury?'

'I can't believe Sophy would ever do such a wicked thing!'

Will shrugged. 'Maybe Andrew died of whatever ailed him, pure and simple. But, right now, Sophy and her mother and sisters are shouting murder, and they're pointing the finger at you!'

'Nobody could possibly believe I'd–'

'Charlotte, they've locked you up and sent for the constable and magistrate!' he cut in, hurrying her as she packed. 'If Hester were here, it'd be different. But she's miles away and won't be back for more than a week. We're servants here! Who's going to pay any mind to what we say when her ladyship's giving the orders? Can you not see I'm afraid for you?' he concluded desperately, clutching her shoulders and staring down into her pinched face. 'If they take you away and lock you up, I'll not be able to help you! I'm just the hired hand!'

Fear suddenly galvanised her into action and, hastily pushing a few more items into the valise, she nodded. 'I'm ready. Wait!' she broke off, gazing up at him. 'Snuffy! What about Snuffy?'

'I've put her in the stable with the wagon pony. She's used to being in there with him. Don't worry, Charlotte, I'll take good care of her.'

He inched open the door, listening before beckoning her to follow him.

Her heart was pounding as she fled along the gallery, past the room where Andrew lay, and down the backstairs.

Liddie was keeping watch in the kitchen passage.

'Quick, miss!' she hissed. 'We've just had the doctor in the kitchen asking all sorts of funny questions about the Master's meals. Hurry up and go before he comes back!'

Clinging to the shadows, Charlotte sped at Will's side across the garden towards the pools of darkness that welled up beneath the stands of old trees beyond the neat lawns.

'I've got Caesar saddled and ready under the big chestnut tree,' whispered Will, clutching her hand as they ran. 'Not far now...'

Holding Charlotte tightly in front of him, Will rode swiftly through the woods, keeping to bridle paths and tracks for as long as possible.

The road into Whitby would've been faster, but carried the risk of confronting the constable and magistrate on their way up to Gaw Hill.

'First chance I get, I'm stabling Caesar,' murmured Will, entering the old town by a dark, twisting ghaut. 'The pair of us riding a horse like him will only draw attention. Besides, too many folk in Whitby know him as Andrew's. That place over there'll do.'

He nudged the horse to veer left, halting outside a livery stables and helping Charlotte down.

'Wait for me over there, by the tea merchant's window.'

She did as she was bidden, shivering uncontrollably as she stood quite alone on the deserted little street, wishing with all her heart that Will would return quickly. Hearing his footfalls upon the cobbles, she turned from the tea merchant's and ran to meet him.

'We'll go the rest of the way on foot and keep to where there're plenty of people.'

He was leading her through an arched ginnel and, taking a purse from his pocket, he pressed it into her hand as they walked.

'Take this and put it safe. It's Hester's. There's enough in there to get you safely to your family, and a bit more besides.'

'I can't take Hester's money!'

'You've no choice, Charlotte,' he snapped, stepping out into a street that was busy despite the late hour. 'Hester told me where she kept that money in case I ever needed it in an emergency. She'd want you to have it. Now, look, that's where we're headed, up yonder. The Gabriel Tavern.'

'I – I can't do this!' She grasped his hand, unable to quell the surge of panic. 'I won't know what to do – I've never even *been* on a coach! I've never been away from Hild

Head before–'

'Hold your nerve, lass!' He fixed her with his gaze, all the while propelling her along the crowded street. 'Everything'll be all right. I'll get you a seat on the next coach leaving town – wherever it's bound!'

At the Gabriel, they squeezed on to the settle along the far wall of the packed coaching inn.

Will was glad of a draught of strong ale, but Charlotte was barely able to swallow a sip of the hot cordial he'd brought her.

'The mail coach for London will leave as soon as they've changed the horses,' he began. 'Then–'

'London?' She stared at him in horror. 'I can't go to *London!*'

'We've not got much time, Charlotte. Listen to what I'm telling you. The coach is bound for London but it passes through York. That's where you get out,' he explained quietly. 'Once you are in York, you'll have to ask when there's a northbound coach to the Lakes. You may have to put up at an inn while you wait. Can you manage to do that?'

He searched her scared white face, and shook his head.

'Charlotte, I cannot leave you like this! I'm coming with you.'

247

'No, Will! You must go back to Gaw Hill,' she interrupted, then she went on, steadily, 'I want you to be there when Hester gets home, to tell her what's happened and where I am. What's more important is that Hester is going to need you. For all their differences, Andrew was her brother, and now he's dead.'

'Yes, she'll need a friend,' agreed Will, adding ruefully, 'The Holcomb Line ... Gaw Hill... I daresay it all belongs to Sophy now, and Hester will be at her ladyship's mercy, Lord help her!'

'Sophy was moving to Egleton, anyway,' Charlotte reflected. 'Do you think she'll still sell the house?'

'Aye, I do– The Holcomb Line and Gaw Hill are up for grabs to the likes of Cristiano Maias,' replied Will in disgust, picking up Charlotte's bag as the coach horn blew. 'It's a rum do, and no mistake!'

Pushing through the throng of jostling customers, they went from the airless, smoky tavern, out into the fresh coolness of the summer night. The sights and sounds and smells of the sea filled Charlotte's senses as she paused a moment, gazing up into Will's grey eyes.

'You'll write, won't you?' she murmured,

touching her fingertips to his rough cheeks. 'You'll let me know what's happening? Thank you for all you've done, I – I'm ashamed to have been so – so–'

'You've done grand, lass!' he whispered thickly, holding her gaze just a moment longer before helping her up into the shining black and red mail coach. 'And don't fret about Snuffy. Like I said – I'll take good care of her!'

Despite the spluttering beams cast by the coach's whale-oil lamps, Charlotte could see nothing from the window as the horses galloped over the moors.

The world beyond the confines of the coach was nothing but an endless black wilderness and even within, she could make out little of her fellow travellers – an elderly couple who, like herself, had boarded at the Gabriel.

She had no idea how much time had passed before the guard sitting atop in the dickey seat blew his horn, and through the darkness she glimpsed the blurred glow of a lantern and heard the creak of hinges as the pike-keeper hauled open the gates so that the London coach might proceed without stopping, the mail being exempt from paying toll.

'We must be at Bibby's Turnpike,' commented the elderly man to no-one in particular. 'Another couple of hours and we'll be at the Black Sheep.'

'Sooner the better, Bill!' replied his wife testily. 'Price they charge, you'd think they'd have decent seats on this coach. I've sat on doorsteps more comfortable!'

The miles disappeared beneath the horses' galloping hoofs until, as the man had said, the mail coach stopped at the Black Sheep Inn.

The elderly couple alighted to stretch their legs, but Charlotte decided to stay put in the dark seclusion of the coach.

Voices carried clearly on the still night air, and two men – travelling salesmen, judging from their conversation with the driver – were wishing to travel to York.

'Only one seat inside,' the driver was replying. 'The other of you'll have to go up on top.'

'That's fine by me; it's Harry's turn to sit up top – I had the windy billet last trip!' guffawed the stouter of the pair. 'You've come from Whitby, haven't you?' he went on. 'Any news of the murder? What? You haven't heard? Well, on our way here we heard about it from a rider who'd stopped at The Old White Bear in Hild Head and had been told about it by somebody who knows the constable. Up at Gaw Hill, it was.'

'Sam Holcomb's old house?' queried the driver, hurriedly climbing back up as time was money where the post was concerned.

'The same,' replied the stout salesman, getting aboard but leaning from the window so that he might continue with his tale. 'It's the old Captain's son who's been murdered! Seems some scullery maid was soft on him but he'd have nothing to do with her, so she poisoned him!

'Talk about biting the hand that feeds you!' he snorted, shaking his head in disbelief and settling comfortably into his seat as the coach lurched onwards. 'The little baggage will hang, for sure!'

Within minutes, the salesman was snoring soundly.

Wrapping her arms tightly across her chest, Charlotte hunched deeper into her corner and closed her eyes.

Sleep, however, had never been further from her.

The salesman's crude and garbled account

of Andrew's death had shocked her from her grief and confusion. Reality suddenly hit her hard.

Suppose *that* was what people believed? Exactly what Sophy had accused her of?

Fighting to gain control of the fearful terror welling up inside her, she pressed her clenched hands to her mouth, forcing herself to remain silent and still when every fibre of her being was aching to cry out and release the unbearable coil of tension tightening within her.

At length, she became aware of blood staining her palms where her fingernails had dug into her own soft flesh, and she gave way to the relief of tears, which were soon coursing down her face.

She'd been branded a murderess.

How could she possibly take such trouble into her sister's home? And surely, if she did seek refuge there, her family would then be guilty of the crime of hiding her?

No, no... She couldn't go to the Lakes and place them in jeopardy.

She'd heard about folk who'd covered up for wrongdoers being sent to prison or transported.

Then she gasped audibly.

Suppose Will–? He'd helped her get away!

Squeezing her eyes tightly shut, she prayed; and as the hours passed, her mind gradually calmed.

During that long, blackest of nights, she carefully gathered her thoughts.

By the time the first light of morning broke into the sky, and the lantern tower of York Minster had come into sight, she had made her plans.

Upon arriving in York, Charlotte bought some breakfast and purchased writing materials from the coaching inn's landlord. She'd already composed the letters in her mind, and had only to put pen to paper.

She was safe and well and would write again. But this was all that she would tell her family, and Will and Hester.

They could not know where she was, nor ever try to find her.

Charlotte was so desperately worried lest they be placed in harm's way through trying to protect her.

The letters were duly sent, and she watched the northbound coach disappear from sight and away towards the Lakes before resolutely returning to the inn and asking the destinations of other stagecoaches leaving York that day.

'Hmm, the Staffordshire coach is due within the hour,' considered the landlord. 'Passes through the towns. Scranton's the first.'

'Scranton? Where's that?'

'Potteries. Small town, but busy. Fifty-odd factories and hundreds of workshops, so I'm told.' He grimaced, as though to dissuade her. 'There's nothing to go there for, miss – unless you want to buy pots!'

Charlotte thanked him, and went outside to await the coach for Scranton.

Her first glimpse of the pottery town was from high up on the Roman road and it was not the buildings or rooftops that caught her eye, but a great pall of dense black smoke the like of which she'd only once seen before, and that had been in a horrific painting depicting Judgement Day.

The stagecoach wasn't carrying mail and did not have the speed of her earlier transportation.

It rattled and juddered past colliery workings, staggering coal heaps, brick pits and smoking engine houses before finally plunging downwards into the depths of narrow alleys and streets, twisting its way through a claustrophobic labyrinth of misshapen, soot-blackened workshops, passageways, galleries and cobbled yards.

Wedged between and amongst these were crooked cottages, outhouses and tumble-down sheds.

Towering over all, however, were gigantic brick chimneys shaped like bottles.

Reaching far up into the sky, they disgorged plumes of choking smoke that blotted out daylight and shed glowing motes of soot into the acrid air.

These settled on to Charlotte's coat and hair when she alighted from the coach, her head tilted back as she stared awestruck at the massive bottle kiln oven rearing up in front of her, just one of dozens that dominated the noisy, teeming town.

She began walking, taking stock of her surroundings and trying to get her bearings. In every corner there seemed to be piles of broken crates, smashed crockery or stacks of heavy containers stacked precariously against walls or tumbled in broken heaps.

Men and women wearing boots or clogs scurried past her in every direction, their heads bowed; barefoot children with grime-streaked faces and ragged clothing darted and dodged; folk shouted at each other in order to be heard above the din of engines, wheels, feet, hoofs and hammering.

Reaching a corner, she hesitated. Which way to go?

The sight of a young mother emerging from a shop followed by two small girls, cramming potato and pie-crust into their mouths, decided Charlotte.

She purposefully strode into the steamy pie-shop with its appetising aromas of gravy and onions.

'Thank you,' she said, taking her purchases and putting the coins of change into her purse. 'I wonder if you might help me? I'm looking for work, and somewhere to live.'

'New to town, are you? Hmm, most folk round here work in the potbanks,' replied the pie-shop woman, scratching her chin thoughtfully as she eyed Charlotte's appearance and manners. 'Don't expect you've worked in the factories before, have you, miss?'

'I'm willing to learn!' responded Charlotte earnestly. 'I really do need a job. Anything at all.'

'Potbanks are your best bet, then,' said the woman, nodding sagely. 'They're busy enough just now and some'll likely be hiring – they mostly want folk who know the trade, of course, but you might try Warrens'...'

Following the pie-shop woman's directions, Charlotte set off and presently approached a high curving wall made up from a hotch-potch of uneven buildings. All shapes and sizes were crammed together, leaning one upon the next and enclosing the works of Warrens' factory.

Reaching a set of huge gates, she tugged at the heavy brass bell-pull. A panel was dragged aside and a stony-faced lodge-keeper peered out, asking her business.

After hearing her out, the keeper sniffed sceptically. 'You seem bright enough. If you're quick on your feet and don't mind getting your hands dirty, the turner might be able to make use of you. He has an order to fill and is down on his number of attendants.'

The panel slammed shut and the massive gates were opened.

Stepping through, Charlotte found herself inside a long brick-built tunnel.

At the far end she could see men shovelling coal, while others disappeared into the walls of the bottle kiln ovens, carrying the same sort of clay containers that she'd seen earlier, balanced upon their heads.

Women and children were swarming in and out of workshops and along tiered galleries like so many bees in a hive.

'By the way, what's your name?'

Charlotte was prepared. She'd already decided to borrow the name of a character from a favourite novel that she and Will had read together.

'Jenny Pearce.'

'Right, Jenny Pearce, I'll take you across to the turner to see if you'll suit. He's in a bit of a pickle today, so you might be lucky!'

The heavy gates swung shut behind her and were locked. Glancing over her shoulder, she realised that all those she loved, and everything dear and familiar to her, now lay outside the potbank walls.

Then, turning to follow the lodgekeeper through the tunnel into the yard, she raised her chin and faced whatever lay ahead.

That Christmas, spent alone, was the hardest of times, but Charlotte wrote home, sending little gifts to the niece and nephew that she'd never seen, being scrupulously careful not to reveal any clues or indication of her whereabouts.

She worked hard at Warrens' and thoroughly learned her job as the cupmaker's attendant, collecting her weekly wage of four shillings and three pence and keeping herself to herself.

And thus her life continued until late one evening when Charlotte, as usual, was amongst the last to leave the potbank.

Only the fireman was still working inside the bottle-shaped biscuit oven, where he'd remain for another day and night, controlling the inferno until the searing temperatures within the kiln soared to twelve hundred degrees celsius and more.

A grey drizzle was falling when she passed through the gates, drawing her shawl over her head and hurrying homewards to her lodgings.

'Charlotte!'

Despite it being almost a year since being called by her given name, she half-turned, before bowing her head once more and scurrying along the cobbles.

But in spite of her haste, the man who'd stepped from the shelter of a doorway to challenge her, easily caught her up, taking hold of her by both of her arms, then stood gazing down at her in wonderment through the slanting drizzle.

'Charlotte – it's me! I've come to take you home!'

'Will?' She stared at him incredulously, then anxiety shot through her. 'Has–'

'Everything is well! Your ma and Lucy and

her family are safe and sound. Snuffy, too,' he reassured her, reading her expressive eyes and impulsively clasping both her cold, gritty hands in his own gloved ones.

'By, I can't believe I'm really seeing you, Charlotte! That you're found at last!'

'How – how did you...?' she mumbled, unable to take her eyes from him. 'What's happened?'

'Everything's grand,' he repeated, a broad smile spreading across his face. 'Just know all is well and you've nothing to fear!'

'Truly?'

'Charlotte, all is well and has been so these past long months. Andrew was judged to have died from natural causes.'

He steadied her as she stumbled, suddenly feeling herself unexpectedly weak at the knees.

'There's so much I need to tell you! Where best can we go to talk?'

'I have lodgings,' she began doubtfully. 'But I share with three other girls from Warren's.'

'I'm booked into the George. They've a nice quiet dining-room and the food's good. We can talk there and have something to eat. You must be hungry after working all day.'

'I'm hardly dressed for dining at the

260

George Hotel, Will!'

'You look just grand to me!' He laughed, brushing a strand of rain-soaked hair from her forehead.

For the first time, Charlotte noticed that Will was dressed in finely tailored clothes and that he was immaculately barbered.

'Come on, lass– Let's get some supper!'

Warmed through by the dining-room's bright fire and relieved of the burden she'd borne since the night Andrew had died, Charlotte gradually relaxed and relished the fine meal; asking all sorts of questions about Will and her family, and about what had been happening back in Hild Head and at Gaw Hill during her absence.

Will's answers and explanations astonished her. She sat on the edge of her seat and listened to him with rapt attention as he spoke.

Only when they were sitting in the softly lit parlour with their coffee did she sit back in her chair and smile broadly at him.

'I can't believe this is happening. I can't believe what you've been telling me – and I can't believe you're here... I was so careful to cover my tracks!'

'If you hadn't been, we'd have found you

261

long ago!' he answered ruefully. 'When I got back to Gaw Hill after putting you on the London coach, Sophy had raised a real rumpus. Folk were poking about the house, asking questions, making notes, searching your room and anywhere else they could think of. Of course, there was nothing to be found and Dr Hawkes swore there was nothing unusual or unexpected about Andrew's death.

'That didn't shut Sophy up, mind you, but without a shred of evidence her howls of foul play didn't wash,' concluded Will. 'I wrote to you at Lucy's, then I received your first letter to me and discovered you hadn't gone to the Lakes.

'Immediately that Hester returned to Gaw Hill, she instructed Arthur Glennister to find you – and his man's been searching ever since.'

'If only I hadn't paid attention to that windbag on the coach!' Charlotte exclaimed despairingly. 'If only I'd gone up to Lucy's like we planned... How *did* Mr Glennister find me?'

'It was because of the Christmas gifts you sent to Lucy's children,' said Will. 'The toy trumpet you sent to your nephew, Jacob, had crumpled newspaper packed into the horn to protect it – a page from the *Scranton Gazette!* Lucy sent it to me; I passed it on to Arthur; and that was the clue his man needed.

'He came to Scranton, visited all the local churches, and made enquiries about a pretty young Yorkshire woman who'd recently moved to the town.' Will paused, unable to suppress the broadest smile. 'And here I am!'

'I've missed you! I've missed you so very much–' Charlotte's words faltered and she lowered her eyes, composing herself before continuing evenly. 'I'm so glad Mr Glennister stopped the sales of the Holcomb Line and Gaw Hill. Losing them would've broken Hester's heart.'

'I reckon it would've,' agreed Will soberly. 'But neither deal was signed and sealed, so Arthur put a stop to them both. Sophy was up in arms because she assumed the company and the house would be hers – we thought so too, didn't we? – but as it turned out, she inherited only Andrew's personal fortune which, given his extravagant tastes, wasn't much by her ladyship's standards.'

'Why didn't she get everything? She *was* Andrew's wife.'

'It turned out Master had put a clause in

his Will. Upon his death, the company and house went to Andrew, and would in due course pass to Andrew's own son. However, if Andrew died without a male heir, the whole lot went to Hester.'

'Earlier, you mentioned she's been poorly,' began Charlotte, her hand briefly touching his.

'Her health's been failing ever since Andrew died,' he replied soberly. 'She's poured all her strength into salvaging the Holcomb Line – Andrew had sorely neglected it and had all but ruined its good name as well as its profits. But since he died, I've been helping her to run the company and, between us, Hester and I have restored it to something her father would have been proud of.'

'You both loved the Captain very much, Will. And cared for the company that meant the world to him' said Charlotte gently. 'How – how serious is Hester's illness?'

'Dr Hawkes is doing all he can. She took the fever this last winter and seemed to get over it, but it's never properly gone,' he explained sadly. 'I've never seen Hester so happy as when she heard you were found, Charlotte. It's like she finally has something to live for again.'

'Poor Hester... It'll be lovely seeing her

again. She was a true friend in need to me.'

Charlotte expelled a breath, raising eyes brimming with emotion.

'I'm going home, Will... I'm really going home!'

'Aye, and just as soon as you like. Tonight, if there's a coach!'

She shook her head. 'I'll write straight away to Ma and Lucy and Hester, but I want to give proper notice at Warrens'. We work in a sort of chain, you see. If one of us isn't there, the others can't do their part of the job which means they can't make their wages!'

'Just as you like.' He grinned. 'But I'm not going back to Hild Head until you're ready to leave with me!'

'There's something else,' she said with a tentative smile. 'I'd like to go up to the Lakes and see Ma and Lucy before I return to Gaw Hill.'

'Then I'll come with you,' he offered diffidently. 'If you wouldn't mind some company...'

'It was wonderful being with them again,' said Charlotte. She was in the airy sitting-room above the gardens at Gaw Hill, and knew from Liddie the great pains Hester had

265

taken to get up and dress so that she might welcome her home properly instead of greeting her from her sick bed. 'I was amazed at how grown the children are. Jacob looks so much like Pa!'

'I thought so, too,' agreed Hester, her usually strong voice frail. 'I've visited Edith and Lucy regularly until recently–' She broke off, her eyes troubled and grave. 'Charlotte, I feel so dreadfully responsible for the pain and suffering that you have been caused. Yourself and Will and your family are the last people in the world I would ever wish to see hurt, yet I feel I could have prevented all that has happened. Indeed, I could have prevented Andrew's death.'

Charlotte stared at her in astonishment. 'But Andrew's death was the result of the injuries he incurred during his fight at the Black Jack Tavern.'

Hester's head moved from side to side despairingly. 'No, Charlotte. Andrew *was* murdered. He *was* poisoned. But by Sophy, not by you! She didn't want him, you see, she only wanted his money. But neither she nor Andrew knew of the proviso in my father's will. I, however, had known about it for years. Known that if Andrew died without a son, everything would pass to me and

266

eventually from me to Will, who I've always loved as the son I've never had. Oh, if only I had passed on that knowledge, then none of this would have happened!

'Charlotte, I have been tortured by my thoughts these last months. Tortured by the knowledge of what Sophy has done – she confessed everything to me in a rage when she discovered that her evil plotting had all been for nought; tortured by the realisation that she will never be brought to justice, because I can prove nothing; tortured by my conscience because – Lord forgive me – I am glad that Andrew is gone where he can cause no more harm to either himself or those about him! But worse than all this, I have been sick with the worry of what had become of you, my dear.'

'Hester, please do not distress yourself so!' cried Charlotte, alarmed and concerned by the older woman's extreme agitation. 'I am indeed shocked by what you have told me about Sophy, but not surprised. And you cannot help what you feel about Andrew's fate. Indeed, he ill-used us all. As for me, I am safe now. What does Will say to all that you have told me?'

'I have told him nothing of all this,' whispered Hester. 'I did not want to burden him with my worries. He has been so distressed and broken-hearted by your disappearance, Charlotte. Indeed, I think it has only been our determination to save the Holcomb Line from bankruptcy that has provided us both with the determination to live!'

'Well, I am back now, so let us put the past behind us and start afresh. You always did your best for your brother, so please cast aside any guilt you might feel about his demise. Andrew died from his illness. Dr Hawkes was adamant about that,' persisted Charlotte gently. 'Apart from Sophy's malicious outbursts, there was never even a suggestion of foul play.'

Hester's breathing was laboured and perspiration beaded her forehead.

Charlotte dampened a clean handkerchief with cold water from the jug and putting one arm reassuringly about her trembling shoulders, gently pressed the cool, soothing cloth to the older woman's flushed face.

'Why don't you rest awhile?' she murmured softly. 'We can talk again later.'

'Yes,' whispered Hester, gazing up into Charlotte's concerned eyes. 'I'll look forward to that. Oh, Charlotte, the sight of you is the best medicine I could ever have been given!'

Walking slowly across the gardens with Snuffy close at her heels, Charlotte's thoughts were still up in the little sitting-room.

As she'd left her to rest, Hester had told her, 'Will doesn't know, but when I'm gone, the Holcomb Line and Gaw Hill will be his. And yours too, if you wish it to be so...'

Wandering across the yard, she made her way over to the stables and found Will there, stroking the bay mare's velvety nose. He looked round as she went to his side.

'Did Sophy marry Ralph Kirrige?' she asked him.

'No, but she's likely still meeting him on the sly somewhere, for she's wed to a baronet old enough to be her grandfather. His estate is next to Egleton, apparently, so between 'em they own half of Wharfedale! And I've heard she's moved her mother and sisters back into the manor-house.'

Charlotte merely nodded, and reached out to touch the mare's neck.

'Will, I've neither seen nor heard the sea in the longest while. Will you walk with me along the shore?'

They strolled in companionable silence from Gaw Hill, through the sun-dappled woods and out on to the cliff path. Snuffy ran ahead of them, and Will helped Charlotte down the rough-hewn steps on to the sand, where she stood for a long while, gazing away into the wild openness of the sea and the sky.

'Will you stay?' he said suddenly, reaching out to turn her towards him, and meeting her eyes steadily. 'Will you stay? Stay here, with me?'

'Always, Will,' she whispered, accepting the hand he offered. 'For always...'

And with Snuffy scampering at the water's edge and darting in and out of the sun-spangled wavelets, Charlotte and Will continued hand-in-hand along the deserted, shell-strewn beach watching the tide's turn.

The publishers hope that this book has given you enjoyable reading. Large Print Books are especially designed to be as easy to see and hold as possible. If you wish a complete list of our books please ask at your local library or write directly to:

Dales Large Print Books
Magna House, Long Preston,
Skipton, North Yorkshire.
BD23 4ND

This Large Print Book, for people
who cannot read normal print,
is published under the auspices of

THE ULVERSCROFT FOUNDATION

... we hope you have enjoyed this book.
Please think for a moment about those
who have worse eyesight than you ...
and are unable to even read or enjoy
Large Print without great difficulty.

You can help them by sending a
donation, large or small, to:

**The Ulverscroft Foundation,
1, The Green, Bradgate Road,
Anstey, Leicestershire, LE7 7FU,
England.**
or request a copy of our brochure for
more details.

The Foundation will use all donations
to assist those people who are visually
impaired and need special attention
with medical research, diagnosis
and treatment.

Thank you very much for your help.